About the author

Huw Langridge was born in 1973, the year his favourite novel was written. Rendezvous with Rama by Arthur C Clarke gave him the motivation and desire to write fiction. Prior to that, a healthy obsession with all things horror had him emulating the work of Stephen King at every available opportunity.

He grew up in London and, during his years working as a global IT troubleshooter for an oil exploration company, Huw travelled to a number of places that enabled him to find inspiration and tone for his stories.

Huw released his first print novel *Schaefer's Integrity* in December 2008. It was published by YouWriteOn and is available at all major online booksellers. Further published short works have appeared in The Ranfurly Review, Reflection's Edge, Jupiter SF and Supernatural Tales.

His short story *Last Train to Tassenmere* received an Honorable Mention in Ellen Datlow's Year's Best Horror of 2009.

In 2010 he released his first short story collection *The Axiom Few*.

Huw lives in Surrey, England with his wife Alison and their young son Oliver.

Website: **www.huwlangridge.co.uk**

Follow Huw on Twitter: **www.twitter.com/huwlangridge**

SPIRECLAW

HUW LANGRIDGE

*Miyese!
Hope you enjoy...
Huw xx*

Copyright © 2011 by Huw Langridge

Book design by Huw Langridge
Cover photograph by Huw Langridge

All rights reserved.

No part of this book may be reproduced in any form or by any electronic or mechanical means including information storage and retrieval systems, without permission in writing from the author. The only exception is by a reviewer, who may quote short excerpts in a review.

ISBN   978-1-4478-3056-6

For Alison

1

The day the word appeared to him again, Kieran Whyteleafe was woken by the sound of the wind. He realised he was awake for a good minute before he opened his eyes; enough time to convince himself that his frightening dream had not been real.

His bedroom was orange. The streetlight outside was shining through a gap in the curtains casting a vertical beam of light on the far wall. It was still dark, and the swaying leaves on the tree in the front garden cast oscillating shadows in the gloom.

The wind outside was fierce and blustery, the gale whipping up and whistling around the house. Kieran could hear the leaves outside swishing along the street, undoing the work of the children who had built piles of them on the way home from school the day before.

The sash window rattled in its frame.

Kieran's face was cold. The heating hadn't come on yet. He was cosy under the covers as long as he didn't move to a colder part of the bed. He twisted his head to look at the clock radio.

4:33

In his dream, he had been confined to a police cell. He was awaiting trial for committing a terrible murder, and to his own horror, he knew he had actually done the dreadful deed. He had known he was guilty and had signed a full confession. In his dream, Kieran had thrown his life away, for the sake of one single act of brutality. And now he was going to hang for it.

He didn't even know who he had murdered, or even how and why. But often in dreams, the fine details of the picture didn't matter. It was the broad strokes, the basic lines and framework; the initial sweeps of the brush on the canvas that forged the emotions that he would carry through to the waking world.

Kieran got out of bed, opened the bedroom door and made his way through the flat to the kitchen to make a cup of tea, which he sipped slowly whilst standing at the window, smoking a cigarette and watching the apple tree at the end of the garden sway back and forth in the relentless gale.

~

Not surprisingly, later that morning, Kieran woke up late for work. He checked the alarm. He'd forgotten to set it.

He hurriedly showered, ironed his shirt and fed the cat. There would be no time for breakfast for himself though.

He was still putting on his tie as he ran for the underground station, and he was totally out of breath when he punched his card in at work

'Sorry I'm late. My alarm didn't go off.'

'I don't believe you,' said Mr Cray, who was the postal supervisor for the office block. Mr Cray sat in his high chair behind his high desk up by the mail entrance, looking down at all the ant workers in the mailroom and signing courier packages in and out. He liked to shout at his subordinates. 'I think you slept through it.'

'It's the God's honest truth,' said Kieran.

'I don't care whose it is,' Mr Cray added, 'Anyway I got Taylor to do your round for you. Lots of boxes. Lucky you missed it. I suggest you buy him a beer.'

'I will,' said Kieran as he ambled across the empty post room past the vacant pigeonholes over to the rest area. He sat down and picked up a newspaper off the coffee table.

'Uh, uh, uh. No. Kieran!' said Mr Cray, clicking his fingers as though he was summoning a waiter. 'Just because you missed the mail round, doesn't mean there isn't work to be done.'

Kieran sighed and dropped the paper back on the table.

Mr Cray was pointing at three storage boxes stacked against the back wall of the post room. 'They need to go into one of the cages in the sub-basement. You can take them down.'

Kieran looked at the boxes. The name on the side of each was Edward Gosnell, along with a code, "R14", which indicated the sub-basement location where Mr Gosnell had requested that the boxes be taken. Aisle R, cage 14. The boxes would probably contain his old documents for the last year, ready for archive. Kieran knew a fair bit about the psychology of data archiving, and he wouldn't have been surprised if Mr Gosnell would never need to look at those files again. But Kieran wouldn't be the one ticking the box marked "Incinerate", so he went to find himself a trolley.

Stepping out of the post room into the main corridor was a little like jumping into a fast-running stream. Even down here in the basement of the huge office building, there were scores of people hurrying along looking like they had been burdened with the most important piece of news ever bestowed upon a messenger. Then Kieran remembered that the subsidised coffee shop was in the basement, and it was about that sort of time when the hordes had dropped off their coats and bags at their desks, switched on their PC's and had a brief natter to the person at the next desk about the weekend they'd just had. Then it's "I think I need a Lattucino", before they go rummaging in their handbags and wallets for the small change they'd emptied the 20p jar out for last night.

Kieran walked against the flow of the river to the next door along; to the room where they kept the trolleys.

'Morning Kieran. Shouldn't you be doing your mail round right about now?'

Tim sat behind the desk by the door in the tiny room. He had a wide grin on his face. There was a radio on the windowsill, playing "Blue Roses" by Prefab Sprout.

Kieran smiled, 'I've worked out a way of getting out of it. I shall name it "waking up late".'

Tim laughed and rocked back in his chair, tapping his pencil on the desk, 'I bet he gave you an earful for that,'

'Well, he let me know it had been noticed. Now I've got to take some flipping boxes to the sub-basement. Can I get a trolley?'

'Over there,' Tim pointed to the corner where a few upright and flatbed trolleys sat. On the radio, Nik Kershaw began to sing "Your Brave Face".

Kieran took the handle of a flatbed and wheeled it towards the door. Tim's phone began to ring.

'I'll have it back in half an hour,' said Kieran. Tim nodded absently as he reached for the phone.

~

The lift door opened to reveal the sub-basement corridor. Kieran pushed the box-laden flatbed out into the semi-darkness. The corridor was ugly, with its whitewashed walls and tasteless brown carpet tiles, some of which had been pulled up, making the going hard for the trolley. A fluorescent bulb was blinking on and off erratically further down the corridor and another was fully on, but most of them weren't. It created a gloomy atmosphere that seemed to fit perfectly well with the musty damp smell that filled the air, and the muffled sound of traffic noise from the street above, filtered through metallic vents and pipes. The smell was familiar to most sub basements in London town. Kieran thought of that smell as the smell of History. Going into a basement or a cellar was like going into the past. It seemed appropriate that he was towing a stack of boxes that were nothing but history as far as their owner was concerned.

At the end of the corridor was a set of swing doors, which opened easily when Kieran pushed the flatbed into them. The storeroom beyond was long and deep, but with a low ceiling. Lined up along one wall were parts of desks, dismantled long ago and left there just in case they might be needed again. Their only crime was to look out-of-date, and now they had been replaced by newer, sleeker, more computer friendly models. Along the other wall was a sink, dusty and unused, and a notice board, with a laminated Health and Safety poster from two years ago, and a couple of rolodex cards pinned up. One trying to sell an inkjet printer for fifty pounds, the other simply had the word "Lucy". Someone had tallied a score of 8 next to her name.

Kieran flicked on the lights and the room danced into life. The storeroom was silent, but for the humming of fluorescent light. The place smelled of recently smoked cigarettes.

He pushed the flatbed trolley around a pile of dexion and rolled it on towards aisle R. He had started at A by the door so it was a good way down. Fifty metres or so further along the lights had not come on, but he could see enough in the gloom to make out aisle R, so he maneuvered the flatbed round the corner and pushed it to the end, where he found cage 14.

He threw the bolt on the door of the steel cage and swung it open. It squealed horribly in protest, as though it was an old creaking joint that hadn't been used for years. There was plenty of space inside to lay the boxes down, and that was what he did, swinging his arms and body back and forth metronomically as he pulled each box off the flatbed and placed it in the rear of the cage.

After the last box, Kieran stopped and listened. He could no longer hear the noise from the street. In the silence it was hard to believe that he was in an office block of three thousand employees. From the sound, or lack of it, Kieran could easily have been in a sub-basement at the end of time, where he was the only man left alive, doomed to live amongst the archive material and the boxed-up discarded history for the rest of his days.

He sat for a moment on the flatbed, pushing and pulling his legs to roll the trolley forwards and backwards under him. He could sit there for a few more minutes and he wouldn't be missed, probably even have a smoke. He looked at the ceiling. No smoke alarms. Handy, though a little stupid considering the amount of paper and cardboard down here. If this place caught fire... well, it didn't bear thinking about.

Still, the cigarette was a good idea. He pulled one straight out of the box in his pocket and lit it with a lighter from the other. The first inhalation was always the best. For that tiny moment, the rest of the world ceased to exist.

Then Kieran saw something behind the cage. He saw it through the chicken-wire mesh that backed onto the cage in aisle Q. The thing that he saw triggered something else in his mind. It was a strange sort of something deep in the part of his memory that he rarely accessed. If his subconscious was divided up into aisles, like a sub-basement in the office block of his life, this aisle would be labeled "Nostalgia", and the cage would be called... it would be called "Unsolved".

Kieran stood up to take a closer look at the thing he saw.

Cage 14 - which now contained the boxes he'd brought down - was at the end of the aisle, and along the side of the cage was a thin walkway that ran along the back of the aisles, but it was barely wide enough for someone to squeeze through.

Just a little further along the walkway was a window. Next to the window was a door that led into an old unused office. Through the window Kieran could see that the lights were off. Perhaps sometime in the past someone running the storeroom would have used the office. But now the only way to get to the door was to squeeze along the tiny walkway that led from the back of aisle R.

No, nobody used that office anymore. The dexion cages had been built in front of it since then.

But it wasn't the office itself that had captured Kieran's attention. It wasn't the beaten up door that was probably locked. No, it was the window that interested him; the window that provided a view out into the storeroom for whoever in the past sat within that office.

On the window was a layer of dust, just like everywhere else in this basement. In the dust, someone had written a word, using a finger as a pen, like a child who writes his name in the condensation on the inside of a car window, or like the rear doors of a van that hadn't seen a sponge and soapy water for a good while, where someone has written "Clean me".

Just like those things, someone had written a word on the window.

The word was "Spireclaw", and he'd seen that word somewhere before.

2

Kieran is hungry, and he is getting tired. The sun is beginning to set and his Mum will be expecting him home for dinner. His best friend Phillip Hynes is going to cycle back with him. Phillip's parents have allowed him to stay the night, so they're going to play computer games and stay up late to watch a horror movie. It is Friday evening, and there will be no school until Monday.

He's in Ealing; at the place the other kids call "Vanguard's". It's a BMX track beside the motorway. It's called Vanguard's because of the factory on the other side of the motorway, which has the word "Vanguard" written on the side. Vanguard is also the name of a computer game that looks great, but he has never played it because twenty-five pounds is a lot of pocket money to save, and Kieran has too much of a sweet tooth to be able to save for that sort of thing. That's five weeks of paper-round money. Kieran simply doesn't have the self-discipline for it. He likes sweets too much.

'Come on Phillip we've got to go. Dinner will be ready soon.'

Phillip is out of breath. He's just done a full lap of the circuit in forty-six point five-three seconds, which is the world record. He stops his bike beside Kieran's and says; 'Let's race one more lap. Then we'll go okay?'

Kieran looks at the sky. The sun is dropping below the houses and the clouds are turning a deep pink and yellow. The light is going, sure. But there is always time for one more lap.

'Okay, but we'll have to bomb it home after. My Mum'll go mad if we're not back in time for dinner.'

Kieran and Phillip race one more lap. Phillip is in front most of the way, but on the big jump down the back straight he lands badly and his bike buckles underneath him. Kieran thinks it's mad, like a stunt out of a film, a stunt that has gone wrong.

Phillip has grazed his knee pretty badly, and he has to pick out all the gravel, wincing each time he puts his fingers near the wound. The cut bleeds down his leg as he limps back to Kieran's house; Kieran riding alongside him as he pushes his bike up the hill.

Phillip wants to go home.

'Don't go home, come back to mine still. We've got plasters and Dettol and we'll sort you out, no fear.'

'I dunno, maybe I should just...'

HUW LANGRIDGE

Kieran is desperate for Phillip to come over and stay. 'You've got to see our cellar. It's absolutely awesome down there. Especially at night. It'll be great, and then we can watch Halloween Two after. Or even better. Before! That'll really freak us out. We can go down there and... well it'll be great.'

Phillip takes some persuading, but he does go round in the end. Kieran's Mum helps them clean up Phillip's leg, on which the little rivers of dried blood have run all the way down to his socks. Kieran loans him a spare pair of socks and trousers and his Mum puts the dirty shorts and socks in the wash so that they are dry by the morning.

~

Kieran is thirteen and his Dad has been dead a year by now. Graham Whyteleafe lost control of his car on a motorway and caused a pile-up. After his death things changed a lot. Kieran's Mum has been different to him. A better kind of different. For his last birthday she'd bought him a bike. It was the best present he'd ever got. Of course he never knew that she had to extend her overdraft to pay for it, pushing her more into the red than she ever wanted to be. It was like the way she paid for the supermarket shopping with a cheque she knew would bounce. It was necessary. It wasn't until many years later that Kieran understood the significance of the bike. That is one of the funny things about being a kid. All this grown up stuff is happening around you, and at the time it doesn't all make sense. But when you look back at some of the events that you don't quite understand, well... viewing them with grown-up eyes often provides a new perspective.

~

After dinner she lets them watch Halloween Two on video. She even lets them move the TV and video into Kieran's bedroom so they can build a camp out of tables and chairs with blankets draped over them and put the TV inside and get all cosy and switch off the lights. The film is scary, and by the time it is finished, Lorraine Whyteleafe has gone to bed.

SPIRECLAW

It is well after eleven o'clock, the perfect time to go into the cellar.

Kieran goes and gets a torch from the kitchen and switches it on to check the batteries are okay. He also gets a large flathead screwdriver. The two of them are wearing their pyjamas, but they have put their shoes on because there is a lot of rubble down there.

The hatch down to the cellar is in the hall near the front door, and it's like the negative version of an attic hatch, where a section of the floor needs lifting out of the way to enable access.

Kieran lifts the piece of cut carpet that fits snugly over the hatch, revealing a chessboard style tiled floor. Then he uses the screwdriver to lever up the section of floor. There is a small area at the side of the piece of floor where the levering has always been done in the past, and the floor is partly worn away by all the activity. But it actually makes it easier to get purchase. Once Kieran has levered the hatch up enough, they ram their fingers into the gap and lift the hatch clear, and lean it against the wall, taking care to be as quiet as possible.

Looking down at the pitch black square that is now part of the floor, Kieran can feel the cold musty air rise up to his face. He is more than a little scared by then.

The two boys look at each other. The fear is rising in Phillip also. It is clear from the look on his face, even though it is hard to see in the gloom. They've just watched a horror movie, and the darkness means much more than just a lack of light right now. But there are two of them, and neither will allow themselves to be branded a chicken.

Kieran points the torch down into the hole, and the light seems to get swallowed up by it. They can see however, that leaning against the wall in the cellar is a small stepladder.

'You first,' whispers Phillip, and Kieran needs no more encouragement. It is his cellar after all. Of course he will have to go first.

Kieran sits down with his legs dangling into the black pit. Then he feels forward for the top of the ladder with his foot. When they connect, the ladder wobbles more than he would have liked. One of the legs is probably resting on a loose brick.

Phillip instinctively grabs Kieran's shoulder to provide him with additional stability as Kieran descends the steps, and soon he is safely at the bottom of the ladder, surrounded by the blackest darkness ever. Michael Myers from Halloween Two could be standing two feet away from him right now, brandishing a long kitchen knife, poised to strike, and Kieran might never know.

Kieran makes the ladder more stable for Phillip, who then climbs down to share the darkness with him.

~

They walk some way under the house, around the brick supports and uneven ground, passing a huge pile of old newspapers and an old Tesco bag. Kieran tries to shine the torch everywhere, to provide them with constant assurances that they are alone in the cellar, and that no demons are lurking at the fringes of the gloom, or behind the nearest pillars. Phillip stays near. Very near indeed. Kieran has the torch. And in the kingdom of the dark, the boy with the torch is King.

Once they are underneath Kieran's bedroom, the two of them sit down on an old purple blanket Kieran placed there on a previous visit.

'Got the bines?' says Kieran.

Phillip produces the cigarettes and matches from his pyjama pocket and they light one each, inhale, and share a silent moment of enjoyment.

'Isn't it great to have a whole cigarette to yourself?' whispers Kieran.

Phillip nods, 'Oh yes. Yes sir. Not to have to deal with someone else bumming the filter. It's always a good thing.'

'I hope you're not saying that I bum the fags.'

'Don't worry I didn't mean you.'

They'd used a letter to buy the cigarettes. Back then the shop owners weren't so hot on catching underage kids buying cigarettes. Most of the time a forged note from your mother is enough to secure the goods.

SPIRECLAW

As Kieran is thinking about this loophole in the cigarette market, toying with the cigarette in his hand, rolling it between his thumb and index finger because it is too girly to hold it between the index and middle, Phillip has taken the torch and is swinging it round like a light-sabre. He is even making the noises. Then he says; 'I'd bet you'd like it if Samantha was here now.'

Kieran smiles and thinks of Samantha. 'Ah Samantha. I'm still getting over that new pink top she wore to school on Wednesday. What I wouldn't give to play spin-the-bottle with that girl.'

Phillip is smiling, 'I don't think Samantha's all that. She's totally flat-chested. Jennifer though. She's developing a nice pair don't you reckon.'

Kieran shakes his head, 'I don't go in for the whole tits thing. And her nose has that strange bump on it. It's more of a man's nose I think.'

'Nah, she's hot. I like her. It would be cool if they were both here right now. Jennifer sitting beside me here and Samantha over there next to you.'

'That would be pretty cool wouldn't it?'

They are silent a little longer and Kieran is thinking about Samantha. He stares at the cherry on his cigarette. Down here in the dark that cherry is like another friend. Another friend with a warm glowing heart.

Phillip is swinging the torch again. But he stops, and a few seconds later he says, 'What does Spireclaw mean?'

Kieran looks up at where the torch is pointing and sees the word. It is written sloppily in thick white paint on one of the brick supports. In the blackness, Kieran's eyes can't help but be drawn to the word. It even seems for a moment that everything around that wobbling circle of torchlight is moving towards it. Like the word is drawing in all the shadows of the cellar.

Just a trick of the dark.

Kieran blinks away the illusion and looks at Phillip. 'Spireclaw. Don't know. I don't remember seeing that there before.'

'Really?'

'Really. I mean. I might have done. It's a weird word though. I'm sure I'd remember.'
'But how many times have you sat down here?'
'Not that many, just a couple of times.'
'And you never saw that word?'
'No. I mean there are some pots of paint down here somewhere. Don't think there's any white though.'
Phillip looks at Kieran, 'Doesn't that freak you out just a little bit? I mean, it's right under your room. Someone could have been down here writing it while you were asleep, just up there.'
Kieran looks at Phillip. Phillip's face is only half visible in the torchlight, 'Freak me out?' He looks around at the dark that surrounds them. Strangely, something about the darkness is beginning to turn. It is rapidly shifting away from being a friendly dark. Now it is just a weird dark. A cold dark. He really hasn't seen that word before. Spireclaw. But he should have seen it because he's been down here a few times now. Could someone really have been sneaking around down here? Doesn't it freak him out just a little bit?
'Actually,' he says. 'Yes it does.'
'Shall we get out of here?'
'That's a very good idea.'
They find themselves moving quickly back to the cellar hatch. Not too quick. They don't want to be branded as chickens after all. But something about the word has chilled Kieran, and Phillip looks equally scared about it. Back at the hatch, they quickly reposition the ladder, and Kieran shines the torch upwards, lighting the way for Phillip, who wastes no time in mounting the steps.
As Phillip climbs, Kieran dares not look around at the enveloping darkness. He dares not try to peer into the immediate blackness that exists just inches away from his face, and stretches away in all directions in the expanse of the cellar. He just looks up at the things that he can see and pretends that he is bathed in light.
But it is too late. An image has found its way into his mind. Perhaps it is a silly image, but it is dark and he is feeling the urgency. Behind him, underneath his bedroom, in

the dark cellar, is a three-foot high dwarf. It is carrying a tall white altar candle to light its way.

Phillip is halfway up the stepladder.

Hurry up Phillip I need to get out too.

The dwarf is fumbling with the lid of a white paint pot with a gnarled hand, his stinking breath forming condensation in the musty air.

Phillip is at the top of the ladder and is climbing out of the cellar, he twists round and reaches for the torch and Kieran passes it to him. Kieran stares wide-eyed into the hallucinatory dark.

The dwarf is dipping a thick brush into the paint. It is the brush that Kieran's mother once used to paint the bathroom a few months back. The dwarf is rubbing the handle and cackling quietly to itself.

Kieran can stand it no longer. If his brain can't galvanise his muscles into movement, then his nerves can. He starts up the ladder.

3

Kieran rode the lift with the flatbed up one floor to the basement level.

He thought about his old friend Phillip, with his slightly asymmetrical face, his mesmeric green eyes and his awkward gangly slump. They'd had some good times back then during the four years they were at school together, and then for a few years after that. That night in the cellar at his house in Highfield Road had been particularly scary for them.

When they both reached nineteen, Phillip took time out from education to travel round the world. He was gone for two years, and after he returned, they didn't really stay in contact, even though they lived just a few roads away from each other. It wasn't that anything in their friendship went sour. It was just that they'd gone in different directions with their lives and had less in common than they used to.

They still met up every few months to shoot the breeze and put the world to rights, but he hadn't seen Phillip for almost half a year now, although a couple of weeks back Kieran had received a postcard in an envelope with a photograph enclosed of Phillip with his cheek pressed against the face of his girlfriend Ashley. The picture was still in his pocket, and he pulled it out to look at it.

Phillip had grown a goatee beard and his hair was wild and his skin was sun-dashed and he seemed to look more like an adult now, as through the beard that now hung from his face existed to cover up the child that was once behind it. Phillip and Ashley were on a beach in the photograph, both of them smiling broadly into the lens and squinting at the sun. The camera was being held by Ashley, her arm extending away from the camera at the side of the picture. The postcard that had accompanied the picture in the envelope had been a "wish you were here" from Fuerteventura. On the postcard Phillip wrote that they should get together after he returned to England.

He had, in fact, returned three days ago.

Remembering their excursion into the cellar of his old house when they were just thirteen, Kieran thought it would be nice to meet up and share a few of those old memories. He decided he would call Phillip later.

He returned the picture to his pocket and took the flatbed trolley back to Tim. Then he headed back to the post room to begin the mid morning round.

The whole area was a flurry of activity. Mr Cray was barking orders at people like a war general orchestrating a complex attack manoeuvre on the front line. The post team had worked together for so long now that they were able to dance and weave around each other with admirable deftness and balletic precision, throwing letters and packages back and forth to colleagues and pigeonholes. By now all the internal envelopes had flooded in from the first mail round and there were fewer large packages and external mail now, as they had all been dished out in the first delivery. Kieran was handed a pile of envelopes to sort into his own set of pigeonholes.

SPIRECLAW

He was responsible for the 4th floor East Block, where the accounts department was located, and in the second delivery to this department he often found himself pushing a trolley load of green and white track-feed dot-matrix printouts, containing long lists of numbers that probably meant something to somebody, but definitely meant nothing to him. Today was no exception. Someone had kindly dumped them onto the table in front of him.

As he loaded them onto his trolley, Mr Cray shouted across the bustling room at him, 'Kieran. Make sure you fill in an archive report for that guy who sent the boxes down. Edward Gosnell. I think he's on the sixth floor. Who's doing the sixth floor? Darren is. Kieran. Give it to Darren. I want it delivered this round.'

Kieran took an archive report from the rack of forms that hung at the back of the post room. Using a half eaten biro that dangled on a sellotaped piece of string that was drawing-pinned to the wall, he filled in the form that would be delivered to Edward Gosnell stating for his records that the three boxes had been placed in R14 on today's date. The report was a formality that informed Mr Gosnell of the extension number to call if he wished to retrieve any of the boxes, and that his department would be contacted on a six-monthly basis to evaluate whether the boxes should continue to be stored or not.

Kieran handed the form to Darren, who took it, read it, and looked blankly at his pigeonholes.

'Edward Gosnell doesn't have a pigeonhole,' he said. 'Kieran. Do you know what department he is?'

Kieran looked at Darren's pigeonhole rack, 'Maybe he's a temp, or here on work experience. Just take it up there and ask around.'

Darren shrugged and slotted the sheet of paper into the front of his trolley. Soon he was gone through the door.

~

Kieran and his buckled red and white mail trolley rode the lift up to the 4th floor. He was sharing the lift with a couple of pink-shirt-wearing self important post-graduate types who seemed to think that the most important thing in the world was how bladdered they got last Friday and how bladdered they were going to get this coming Friday. They got off on the third floor, and the smell of Hugo Boss followed them out.

As Kieran pushed his trolley past the regular crowd in the accounts department, saying hello and dropping off piles of envelopes and track-feed paper, his mind wandered to that time he and Phillip were in the basement in the house back in Ealing. Back to the time he first saw the word Spireclaw.

The word itself conjured an image in his mind of an old church, deep in the forest, beaten and weathered by centuries of wind and rain. Only accessible by an overgrown path that folk were too afraid to use at night. And perched atop the church's most elevated cross, a dark bird with a deformed beak. A crow that scanned the stormy land looking for carrion, squawking up at the wind and clouds.

His overactive imagination had created the dwarf in the cellar all those years ago, but the word itself was real; he had Phillip to verify that. And now it had reappeared here, at his work. This ghostly graffiti tag, and both times below street level.

Kieran found he was picking up just as much mail as he was delivering on his round. The company was being audited and the accounts department was busier than ever. When he returned to the post room, his trolley was creaking under the weight of boxes and paper.

Darren bounded up to him as he entered, 'Kieran, there's no Edward Gosnell here mate. I asked around on six. They had no idea who I was on about.'

'Really?' said Kieran. 'Well he managed to dump three boxes down here this morning.'

Darren picked up the office directory that was lying on the postbench and flicked through the pages. 'G, G, G. Here we go.' He ran his finger down the page. 'Geffen, Godber, Gosling, Grimstead. There's definitely no Gosnell here mate.' He flapped the book closed. 'I suggest you call reception and get the temp list.'

'Thanks for trying anyway D.'

Kieran approached Mr Cray's desk. Mr Cray was coming to the end of a phone call that consisted of him yelling while the person on the other end listened. '...and we are paying you to see that it is!' he barked into the receiver, which he then dropped back on the cradle. He looked up at Kieran. 'What do you want?'

Kieran presented the archive report to Mr Cray. 'This Edward Gosnell fella. D's been up to the sixth and tried to deliver this form and they don't know who he is.'

Mr Cray snatched the sheet of paper from Kieran. 'Must be thinking of someone else. Is he in the directory?'

'No, I was wondering if you had a copy of the temp list.'

Mr Cray gave a rare smile, though it was more of a smirk. 'Yes I do.'

He shuffled a few loose papers around on his desk. Courier airwaybills and ripped open jiffy bags, a good many of which were adorned with harsh, angular biro doodles. Three-dimensional cubes and spirals drawn over and over so many times that the paper was nearly torn. He found the temp list and scanned the names on it.

'Were you here when the boxes arrived, Mr Cray?' said Kieran.

'Nope. They were here before I arrived, which was about two hours before you got here, I seem to remember.'

Kieran didn't allow himself to be roused by the jibe. He remained quiet.

'Nah, he's not on here either,' added Mr Cray.

'So what should I do?'

Mr Cray screwed up the archive report and tossed it into the bin behind him. 'Obviously a clerical error. I'd say bollocks to it.'

~

Kieran and Darren spent lunch together in the little park by Temple underground station, wrapped up in coats against the October chill, eating Pret sandwiches, drinking tea from paper cups, and watching the pretty girls come and go from the office.

'So I'm wondering if that was a sensible idea,' said Kieran. 'Cray chucking it in the bin like that.'

'Why?'

A river bus on the Thames carrying a handful of tourists sounded a loud horn. The sound was soon lost amidst the embankment traffic noise and the sound of heels belonging to the dozens of passers-by in Temple Gardens.

'He called it a clerical error. I'd say it was a bit more serious than that. I mean. Those boxes appeared out of nowhere, and now I've stuck them in the sub-basement. Aren't we all supposed to be really hot on security now? God only knows what's inside them.'

Kieran looked around the gardens. At this time of day every bench displayed the same picture. Young men and women in business attire balancing cans of drink and sandwiches on the bench arms and their legs, trying to read a paper or take in the scenery. The wind was still gusty from the morning, but nowhere near as bad as it had been in the dawn hours. Most of the clouds had parted now, and the air was crisp and fresh. The autumn sun cast long tree-shaped shadows across the leafy lawn.

'Does the word "Spireclaw" mean anything to you?' said Kieran.

'Spireclaw? No, I can't say it does mate.'

Kieran nodded, 'Hmm. Didn't think so somehow.'

'So, what did the boxes feel like? Were they heavy?'

'Yeah, they were heavy. Well, two of them were heavy. The other one felt like it was empty, but something was rattling around inside.'

Darren uttered a thin laugh, 'I doubt if any of them were bombs though.'

Kieran nodded, 'I know. But it's strange don't you think? The way they turned up like that. Sent down by someone who doesn't exist in the company. It's one of those things that nags at your mind, like.'

'If it's nagging at your mind, why don't you go back down and check them out? Put your mind at ease,' said Darren.

'Okay,' Kieran said absently, 'Gonna call Phillip first though.'

~

There was a quiet ten minutes after the lunch break, before the first of the two afternoon mail runs. He knew that in that time Cray wouldn't miss him.

He nipped into the post room and dialed Phillip's number on the Cray's phone while Cray was still at lunch.

Phillip's number was engaged.

Kieran hung up and went out the door into the lift. He pressed the button for the sub-basement, following the route he had taken just a couple of hours before. Soon he found himself in the storeroom, walking along aisle R to the end, where cage 14 sat.

The three boxes looked ominous this time, but his curiosity would not let him back out now. He had to find out what was in them, just so that he could let this little mystery rest.

Kieran opened the cage and walked in. As he approached the first box he dug into his pocket for his house-keys. He used one of them to cut the brown tape that held the box shut, getting his fingers tacky as he pulled it away in twisted ribbons.

For a moment he felt a sense of wrong in his mind. Should he really be digging through someone else's things in this way? What if he got caught? What if Cray found him?

Kieran stopped and listened to the room. All he could hear was silence. If anyone came along, he would hear them coming, and he would have plenty of time to hide or put the boxes back as he found them.

He lifted the lid off the box and put it to one side.

Inside was a pile of newspapers, tied together with string. They were old copies of The Times dated Friday October 15th 1943. Kieran lifted up a corner of the top paper, and he could see that all the newspapers in the bundle were the same. There were about twenty of them. The headline on the front read: GERMAN FORCES WITHDRAW FROM DNEIPER'S EAST BANK

Kieran cut through the tape on the second box and flipped open the lid. Inside were more newspapers, also dated Friday 15th October 1943.

He moved onto the third box, the empty one, and then stopped, listening.

Footsteps, outside in the corridor. His nerves jumped. He remained absolutely still, unbreathing. The footsteps were getting quieter. The person sneezed. Kieran heard the lift doors. Then silence.

He cut through the tape on the third box and opened the lid.

Inside was an audiocassette. Kieran took it out and turned it over in his hands. The clear case showed a very old inlay card. This cassette looked like it was bought in the 1970's. It was a blank cassette, or at least, it had been bought as blank. Kieran knew it had been recorded on though, because the protectors on the top had been snapped off so nobody could record over it again.

No one had taken the time to write what was recorded on it, either on the tape itself or on the inlay card, so the only way to know what was on it was to listen to it.

Kieran stood up and surveyed the mess he'd made. Then he remembered the time.

'Christ!' he'd been gone much longer than ten minutes. It was more like twenty-five. Cray would probably hang him for this.

He hastily replaced the lids on the boxes, not caring about refastening the tape. He'd made such a mess when pulling the sticky tape off that he would never be able to get it back on properly anyway.

Kieran looked down at the audiocassette in his hand. He knew he was faced with a decision.

He thought for a moment about the cassette.

He put it into his pocket, smiling to himself about just how nosey he sometimes could be.

~

SPIRECLAW

Kieran switched off the television, giving silence back to his flat. He picked up his dinner plate and carried it through to the kitchen, where he scraped the uneaten remains of beans on toast into the bin. He dropped his plate into the sink.

Gandalf was sitting in his favourite place on the windowsill looking out into the night. He made a vocal purr of surprise and looked round when Kieran stroked his soft white mane.

He tried Phillip's number again on the telephone. The line was still engaged.

He flicked open his address book to the letter H and scanned the numbers in the list. Then he picked up the receiver on the kitchen phone and dialed the number for Phillip's mother's house.

It rang six times at the other end, and Kieran was just about to hang up when he heard a click.

'Hello?' said a quiet female voice.

'Mrs Hynes. Good evening I'm sorry to disturb you. I hope I haven't rung at a bad time.'

'Hello? Who is this? No it's okay love, I can handle it. Hello? This is Mrs Hynes.'

'Hello, Mrs Hynes. You might not remember me, my name is Kieran Whyteleafe. I was a friend of Phillip's at school.'

'Oh. Oh my!'

'In fact, I was wondering if this was still your phone number. The phonebook I've got is about three years out of date. I'm ever so glad you're still at this number. It's just that I've been...'

'Kieran. Kieran Whyteleafe yes. Yes I remember you. Good God Kieran, why did you call today?'

Gandalf started to brush his nose against Kieran's leg.

'I'm sorry? I was actually wondering if there was a problem with Phillip's telephone. I've been trying to call him and it's been engaged all day.'

There was a fumbling at the other end of the line. The receiver was being passed to someone else, Diane was sobbing.

'Hello Kieran this is Arthur.'

'Hello Arthur. Is everything...'

'Kieran? Did you know?'

'Did I know what? I'm sorry. Perhaps I have the wrong number for him. I don't think I do but...'

'Phillip's dead. He committed suicide. He was found dead this morning.'

Silence

'What?'

Silence.

'He's dead Kieran. That's why it's a surprise that you're calling.'

'What happened? I mean... how?'

'Ashley, his girlfriend. She was working late at the studio. She didn't get back to the flat until the early hours. She found him. In front of the television. He poisoned himself.'

~

Kieran hung up the phone. Yes he would go to the funeral. Yes she should call him and let him know what date it would be. Yes he was very much looking forward to seeing her again and filling in the gaps made by the years between. Yes Phillip would have liked that.

Kieran sat on the floor in the middle of the kitchen, smoking a cigarette and staring at a single piece of stitching in the jeans he was wearing. The only sounds he could hear were the ticking of the clock in the hall and the wind outside. It was getting up again. It was going to be another blustery night. The forecast said there would be rain.

Gandalf trotted up to him, rubbed his nose against Kieran's knee, and miaowed pathetically for some food.

4

The next morning he was up early. The bright October sun was streaming in through the window and, had the circumstances been different, the day would have been glorious. The leaves on the ground outside were golden brown,

SPIRECLAW

a colour that seemed to fit perfectly with the green grass they lay upon, and the rich clear blue sky above.

After a long shower Kieran went into the kitchen to brew up some coffee. He placed a couple of muffins in the toaster. Gandalf was sitting by the fence at the end of the garden. Upon seeing Kieran enter the kitchen, he thundered up the garden, bounced through the cat-flap, and hovered around his bowl.

'How come I only ever see you when you want food? You little rotter.'

He opened a can of Whiskas and forked three-quarters of the contents into Gandalf's bowl. Gandalf wasted no time in digging in, and making a lot of noise while he went about it.

Kieran stretched back to a standing position, and noticed his trousers hanging over a chair by the table. He'd thrown them there to put into the wash, but now he remembered what was in the pocket.

He put his hand inside the front pocket and pulled out the audiocassette. Turning it over in his hands he wondered if anyone would miss it, at least for the time being.

He took the cassette out of the case, placed it in the tape player he had in the kitchen, and pressed Play. The tape stopped straight away. He ejected it and turned it over, and pressed Play again.

~

After the leader, there is the sudden sound of a baby, uttering a long happy wavering noise that sounds like he or she is being bounced on someone's knee.

A man's voice speaks over the baby, 'Up and down, up and down.' The man sounds sort of middle aged, perhaps older. But it is no voice Kieran can recognise. But then, why would it be?

The man is making up a rhyme for the baby. 'Can-you see-the boats, out on-the sea? Can-you see-the boats?'

Now a woman's voice, she sounds middle aged too, and with no discernable accent, 'I've got to go up to the shops. We need milk and flour. I don't have enough to make this cake.'

'Okay Darling,' says the man.

She carries on, 'And I need hundreds-and-thousands. Now have I got enough Bourneville? Oh dear I'd better make a list.'

'No need to get in a flap my love there's plenty of time,' says the man in a calm, reassuring voice.

Strange unintelligible rumble noise, far away.

'Ooh look, look at that!' says the man.

'Where?'

'Over there. Between the houses. It's down.'

'Oh yes. Gosh I hope nothing's wrong.'

'Beautiful. It's quite majestic when you see it like that isn't it? Not when you just...'

'Yes... yes...' she says dreamily, 'Anyway, I really must go. Shall I take him with me?'

'Yes, why not.'

There is a pause, and then the man utters a strained sigh, like he is struggling to get out of his chair.

A few seconds of rustling. A door closing. It isn't an outside door though. It's inside, like a bedroom or a bathroom door.

The woman, whispering, 'Pass him here.' Then louder, to the baby, 'Hello little you.'

The man says, 'How long do you think you'll...'

'Ooh not long, just twenty minutes or so.'

More rustling, a floorboard creaking under the carpet.

She speaks again, 'See you later.'

'Bye love,' the man says.

A door slams shut. Footsteps dying away outside. A car door opening.

Inside, soft footsteps walking around.

Silence. The occasional deep breath. A cough.

A car driving off outside.

Rustling, then a flapping noise. The sound of wood scraping against wood.

A light thud, like the sound a wooden spoon would make if it were hit against a chopping board.

Fumbling, fumbling, fumbling. Another cough.

The recording stops, the tape goes blank. Now only the high-pitched hiss of unused tape.

SPIRECLAW

Stop. Fast Forward. Stop. Play. Nothing. Stop. Fast Forward. Stop. Play. Nothing.

~

Kieran stood in the sub-basement at the office. Here he was again, looking at the boxes. He was holding a pair of scissors. There was no one around.

Right now he was finding it easier to concentrate on the mystery of the archive boxes than it was to think about Phillip. His reaction to Phillips suicide had yet to form correctly in his mind. The whole idea was still sinking in. And while he was numb to the news, Edward Gosnell's archive material was a beguiling diversion.

He lifted the lid off the first box again and snipped the string that bound the old newspapers together. Then he took the top paper off the pile. It was faded and brown, and the paper felt old and rough, not smooth like today's newspapers. He carefully folded it into the copy of the Metro newspaper he was carrying, and then replaced the lid on the box.

Now there would be no doubt that someone had tampered with the boxes. If Edward Gosnell decided to check out his archived material he would get quite a surprise. But for some reason, Kieran had come to the conclusion that Edward Gosnell wasn't going to be showing up anytime soon.

But why? Kieran thought to himself as he closed the door on cage 14. What possible knowledge did he have about the elusive Mr Gosnell. Just because his name didn't show up on the office extension list. Just because nobody on the 6th floor knew who the man was. So what? There could be any number of ways that an error could have been made. And even then, it certainly didn't give Kieran the right to go rooting through those boxes for no apparent reason. And what had he found? Well it wasn't a bomb of course. There was no security issue. All it was was just a bunch of old wartime newspapers and a stupid cassette of some woman talking about going to the shops. Altogether not the most riveting of archive material. Okay, maybe it all meant something to Edward Gosnell. Maybe he was archiving some research material, or some family heirlooms. The point is, it was none of Kieran's damn business.

He let out a deep sigh. Maybe it was time he let it go. After all, there were other things to occupy his mind now. More important things like the suicide of his old school friend. Perhaps he really should be starting to allow the grief in.

Kieran paused, almost ready to turn around and return the newspaper to the box.

No. It can wait till tomorrow.

He headed off towards the lift.

Tomorrow, after he had looked at the newspaper he would bring it - and the cassette - and return them both to the box.

~

Kieran returned home from work at the usual time of 6:45pm. In the cold sky the sun had almost set, but the high pink cirrus clouds gave the world a wonderful heavenly glow.

Gandalf met him outside the front door, eager to get inside. Kieran could think of only one reason why. Cats were after all just little four-legged eating machines.

He switched on the light in the kitchen.

The audiocassette was lying on the floor. The tape had spooled out all over the floor, and Kieran could see it had snapped.

'Oh Gannndalllfff! You bloody stupid cat.'

Gandalf was waiting at his bowl.

'Did you do this? Did you do this?'

Gandalf started to clean under his armpit.

Kieran dropped his bag and bent to pick up the tape. Holding it in both hands he looked closely at it, trying to ascertain whether it could be mended. Then he started to wind the broken tape onto one of the spools.

The telephone rang. He answered it quickly, placed the receiver between his ear and shoulder, and continued to spool the tape.

'Hello?'

'Kieran, this is Diane Hynes, Phillip's mother.'

'Oh, yes, hello. How are you keeping? Is everything...?'

'Yes, everything's fine. Everything's in order.'
'Good, good.'
'Listen, Kieran I just wanted to let you know that the funeral will be a week on Friday if you would still like to come.'
'Of course I do. Of course. What time?'
'It's at two o'clock, at the Breakspear Crematorium in Northolt. Do you know where that is?'
'I should be able to find it.'
'Okay, well, that's two o'clock then.'
'I'll see you there, Mrs Hynes. Thank you for calling.'
'Goodbye.'
Kieran replaced the receiver, and stared down at Gandalf, 'I can't believe it little fella. Can you? Phillip Hynes eh? Phillip bloody Hynes is dead.'
Gandalf pounced up onto the sink and deftly navigated his way past the mug-tree to his favourite spot on the windowsill, where he settled down and looked out at the cold evening.

~

After dinner, Kieran poured himself a straight double Jack Daniels and sat at the kitchen table. He brought the old newspaper out of his bag and flattened it out in front of him. Then he pulled the Concise Oxford Dictionary off the bookshelf in the lounge and laid it next to the newspaper. Gandalf jumped up to see what he was doing, then curled up into a ball at the edge of the table and pretended to sleep.

Kieran looked at the old text before him. There were two major stories printed in The Times on October 15th 1943, the first being the story under the headline about the German Army's retreat from the Zaporozhe bridgehead on the bank of the Dneiper River. The second story detailed the heavy attack delivered by the US 8th Air Force against the ball bearing plants in Schweinfurt, and how the Luftwaffe lost only forty planes compared to one-hundred and ninety-eight of the US's B-17's.

Kieran took a sip of whiskey and lit a cigarette. Gandalf was purring softly with his eyes closed.

He took the dictionary and searched for Spireclaw.

No such word.

He put the dictionary away and reached for the phone directory. Flipping through the pages he found the letter G, and read down the page.

No Gosnells in West London.

Kieran picked up the phone and dialled directory enquiries.

It didn't matter that he didn't have an address for Edward Gosnell. There were no Gosnells listed on this green and pleasant land anyway. For some reason this didn't surprise Kieran in the slightest.

'No Gosnell's,' he said to himself after putting the phone down. 'No Gosnell's listed in the UK,' as though the very act of saying it confirmed the obscure revelation in his mind.

He returned to the table and opened the newspaper to the next page. Here there were more details on the two cover stories.

He turned the pages forward until he reached the births, marriages and deaths section. Perhaps Edward Gosnell's name would be written somewhere there. An all-revealing obituary perhaps. He spent a few minutes reading the names. No sign of Edward Gosnell.

Kieran closed the paper. What was he looking for? Why was he looking for it? Would there really be something in this newspaper that was connected to Edward Gosnell? And what of the cassette? Just because the cassette was in a box that was stored with the newspapers, did that mean that there would be a link? Perhaps this Gosnell bloke just happened to archive the items at the same time, and there was no link between the tape and the newspaper at all. And what if Gosnell was storing the newspaper for someone else? What if it was one of those "date of birth" newspapers? There was nothing to indicate that the newspaper would contain Edward Gosnell's name.

Or was Kieran looking for the word. Was he looking for Spireclaw?

But that's just ridiculous.

And if the word Spireclaw did turn up somewhere in these aged pages, what exactly would that mean? There was nothing to connect Spireclaw to Edward Gosnell and the newspapers, or Spireclaw to the cassette. It was just an unrelated word that Kieran had seen in the basement at the same time.

But he couldn't banish the feeling that someone or something wanted him to see it.

Kieran took a final tug on his cigarette, inhaled deeply, and stubbed it out in the ashtray. 'Gandalf, I think I've gone completely mad. I'm chasing shadows.'

He sat back, folded his arms, smiled and shook his head. He was looking too hard at something that just wasn't bloody there. The only associations between all these things were in his mind.

It really was time he laid the whole thing to rest, and returned everything back to its rightful owner.

Just as soon as he got the tape fixed.

5

My hands and feet are numb with cold. We have been standing here for two hours. We are not allowed to move.

I look up at the jagged line of evergreens in the Parczew Forest beyond the fences and I wish I could stand among them. I want to feel the rough bark of their trunks with my hands because it is natural. It is natural, and this is not. Some of the trees are wounded, their branches snapped away and threaded into the fences to camouflage the camp from the outside world, and conceal parts of the camp from each other.

We are standing on the Rampe. Hard concrete and slippery leaves underfoot. Behind us is the train that brought us here from Lublin. We are separated into groups. The men are in one group, and women with small children in another. I can see my wife. She is wearing a heavy brown full-length coat, given to her by a friend before we were herded into the ghetto. She looks terrified. She is scanning the lines of men, looking for me, but she doesn't see me. I dare not wave. I daren't move a muscle. But I will her to see me. Her eyes dart left and right and still she does not spot me.

Suddenly there is a lot of shouting. The guards are telling people to hurry.

The huge train behind us blows its loud resonant whistle and begins to haul itself away. Twelve long dark carriages smelling of putrid human waste. Urine and death. My wife and I travelled for two days in that awful train. All the time there was shouting from the sidings. "Jews, you are going to your stinking death!" I never want to see that train again. For one reason or another, I am sure I never will.

The guards lead us forward along the schlauch, a walkway that leads to an area they call Lager Zwei, or Camp II. The buildings there are many but each is low and identical to its neighbour. Wooden huts that seem barely able to stay standing, let alone keep out the bitter Siberian wind.

Looming above us to our right is a watchtower. There are two guards up there. They are Blackies; Ukrainian guards. They are holding semiautomatic Mausers. They are looking down to an area behind the building that is in front of us. They are smiling.

My rapid fearful breath forms condensation around my face. There are at least a hundred of us in our lines, and we are all as scared as each other. I am afraid for the women, and the children. I am afraid for myself, but I am more afraid for my wife, because I love her more than anything in the world, and her happiness, her life, is more important to me than my own.

I look nervously around my group of men. We are all tired from the train and thin from hunger.

From behind Lager Zwei, I hear a single rifle shot, and it shocks a cluster of birds from the trees. They take flight, silhouetted against the grey morning sky.

Further away to the left I can hear frantic squawking. They say the guards keep geese at Sobibor.

'Entfernen Sie Ihre Kleidung' shouts a guard to the crowd of women, and they obey, even though it will be cold for them. One of the guards snatches a bracelet from a woman' wrist. He tosses it into a pile of valuables retrieved from the other people in the assembled crowd. A young woman is clutching a photograph to her breast. I cannot see what the picture is. The guard snatches at it, tearing the photograph. The woman lets

SPIRECLAW

out a cry. I see a guard with an evil smile snatch my wife's necklace. The chain breaks. It is a beautiful gold piece. I made it with my own lime-stained hands. If the guard were to open the little heart-shaped door on the pendant, he would see a picture of my wife and I in happier times. It is the only photograph of us that we possess, except, now we don't possess it.

Soon the women are fully naked. Dignity stripped from them as easily as clothes from their frail bodies. I realise that I am crying.

Somewhere in front of us, on the other side of the camp, there is another line of people. They did not come from the train, and I cannot see them, but I can hear them. There are guards shouting orders to them.

A door opens in a building near Camp III. A few of us turn our heads to look. A line of women emerge. Their heads are shaved. There must be about fifty of them. They are walking slowly around the back of a larger building. The guards are telling them to hurry, that their work awaits them.

'Schauen Sie vorwärts!' shouts one of the guards near us, and we quickly snap our heads forward. We don't need to be told twice.

I wonder where the women might be working. There seem to be only a few buildings over towards Camp III. Perhaps they will work in the fields behind the camp.

An SS guard walks along the line in front of us. He shouts, 'Tailors? Goldsmiths? Painters? Step forward.'

Some men step out. I wonder whether it is best to remain in line, or step forward.

I decide to go, 'I am a goldsmith.' I say.

Those of us that have stepped forward are taken to a shed where we are given coffee and bread. I take a sip of the hot liquid. It tastes of turpentine. The Jew who gives it to me tells me that the bucket the coffee was taken from had been used to clean paintbrushes.

After we have eaten, we are led out of the hut and taken to the adjacent building. It is a barracks. When I see that I am being shown my bed, a wave of relief hits me.

At least I will not die today.

6

Kieran's flat was situated in a quiet corner of Ealing, in an area called Northfields. It was a nice enough part of the world, even though the rent was expensive, and the journey into London by underground was more than a little hassle. He could think of many worse places to live.

The area felt comfortable for him. It was near where he grew up, and it still felt like he belonged there, even though his family was no longer any part of the area anymore.

After his father died, Kieran's mother remained single for a good seven years. It was just as Kieran was preparing to leave home and get a place of his own (by this time he was nineteen, and eager to make the leap into independence) when his mother met a man from South Africa. His name was Pieter.

A couple of years later, Lorraine Whyteleafe married Pieter and moved out to Cape Town with him. She always made it clear to Kieran that if he ever wanted to chuck it all in and leave London, she would buy him a ticket on the next plane out faster than he could pack his belongings, and Cape Town could be his new home.

Kieran had no intention of moving to South Africa. London was his home and he couldn't imagine a life outside of it. He had not travelled much in his life, just a two-week beach holiday in Corfu and a weeklong camping trip in France. He freely admitted to anyone who would ask that his lack of worldly experience was no doubt a major factor in his reluctance to ever want to leave England.

So he persevered in his Northfields ground floor flat, working in the post room of a large multinational consultancy company, waiting for his big break, whatever that would be.

And it was this flat which he closed the door of on the day of the funeral at a little after noon and walked to the end of the road to catch the first of three buses that would take him to the gates of Breakspear crematorium in Northolt. He wore his black work suit, and a black tie, which he borrowed from

Darren, and though his shoes were scuffed they were the only pair he had.

Sitting on the bus he watched young women with prams and small children loading shopping bags into cars. He watched young men in suits walking in and out of record shops. He watched a group of kids dodging school to sit in the park and smoke cigarettes. All these things he saw were the hallmark of a weekday. The kind of things you don't see when you're at work. These things reminded you that you had the day off.

And usually that would be a good thing. Being off work. But not this time because Phillip Hynes had killed himself, and Kieran didn't know why. As far as he was aware, nobody knew why. But then, did there always have to be a reason? Okay, yes there's always a reason, but was it always possible for others to know the reason and understand?

Perhaps not this time. Kieran toyed with the idea in his mind. What if he never found out why Phillip poisoned himself? It was perfectly possible that the answer would never surface, but would he be able to live with that?

Each time Kieran waited for another bus he smoked a cigarette, all in preparation for the uncertainties that lay ahead. He was going to a funeral where he would probably know only two people. Phillip's mother and father. And it had been nearly ten years since he'd seen them. What would he say?

As for Ashley? He'd only seen a picture of her. He doubted he would get a chance to speak to her at all.

Bright sunshine illuminated the inside of the bus to Northolt, and Kieran found he shared the ride with an old lady who was sitting near the front. In one hand she held a shopping bag while the other hand held a bar for support while the bus leaned sharply around corners. Otherwise he was alone. He felt like he was on a bus to the end of the world.

The bus swept past the Polish War Memorial and on towards the crematorium.

Looking out of the window at the cars and the road, and the flashing that the sun made in his eyes as it flittered through the trees, Kieran's eyes filled with tears, which he thought would stay only in his eyes, but instead escaped to land on his leg like ink on blotting paper.

He hadn't thought to bring any tissues.

~

Breakspear Crematorium was set back from the main road like a stately home, with trees obscuring the view from the gate as though the farewells that were said there were secret and not for the rest of the world to see, lest those people be reminded of their fragile mortality.

Kieran recognised Diane and Andrew Hynes instantly, but they didn't recognise him. This, Kieran supposed was understandable given that he was likely to have changed far more in ten years than they had.

They thanked him for coming, and he followed them into the building.

It was the most modern and drab of churches, lacking any of the character of a real period church. This seemingly functional place made Kieran feel sad, as though those who were laid to rest here were not worthy of a more beautiful building.

Kieran sat at the very back. He only felt able to observe, not participate. The coffin that lay pathetically at the front was as near as he wanted it to be.

Looking around at the other pews he could see about fifty people in attendance, but looking at the backs of their heads it was impossible to tell if any of them were from the school he and Phillip had attended.

When the ceremony began he found he wasn't really listening to the sermon. He found his mind wandering to the best time he and Phillip had ever had. It was the night of the school disco in the last year of primary school. They were thirteen again. It was the night of the double kiss.

~

Tears for Fears have started to play the opening piano chords of Head over Heels and it's definitely Kieran's favourite song.

SPIRECLAW

It's a song that empowers him and he asks Samantha to dance. Ask him in the morning how he had the nerve to do that and he won't be able to tell you, but right now the music and the lights and the fact that it's a warm summer's evening mean he is capable of anything and everything.

Samantha is wearing a floral dress that is making all the boys wish she were on their arm. Her hair is down and it's shining. She's full of colour. She's radiant, and she's dancing with Kieran.

She's looking into his eyes and he has his hand on her soft arm and he hopes this will go on forever. It doesn't get any better than this.

This is the first time he has ever danced with a girl and they're both feeling the song. He can tell she likes it too. Kieran can feel eyes burning into his back. For once the other boys are jealous of him, and it's a beautiful feeling because he knows that his social status has been elevated for good. Nothing will knock him down now.

When the song ends they find themselves outside in the playground, at the back, near the tall oak trees, sitting on the low wall sharing a plastic cup with lemonade in it. The stars are out and it seems like the universe is shining just for the two of them.

They talk about some of the other couples that seem to have gotten together that evening, and then they kiss. This is his first kiss and Kieran is surprised to feel how soft her tongue is. He expected something... rougher. The sensation turns out to be a thousand times more amazing that he ever thought it would be.

The fabric of her dress is smooth to his touch and she smells so exquisitely sweet. He can also smell the summer grass. This moment will frequent his future journeys into his past memories. It will be his favourite.

They kiss a while longer, and when he pulls his mouth away and turns his face to take in the evening once again he sees that Phillip is sitting further along the wall, with Jennifer.

They are kissing, and Phillip's hand is down at his side, he is making a thumbs-up sign directly at Kieran.

And now they are both fully aware of how great things are at that very moment. How the two of them had dreamed this moment would come. And somehow it has. The stars and planets have aligned themselves this evening, and the universe is taking a bow.

Later on that evening, when Phillip and Kieran are alone outside together once more, just before the last of the slow songs begin, just before they go inside to share a final dance with those two girls, he says 'Kieran, I am in Heaven.'

~

'Kieran? I'd like you to meet Ashley Henderson.'

Ashley Henderson was wearing a conservative black dress and business style suit jacket. She was pretty, and Kieran could see why Phillip would have gone for her. She smiled as she shook Kieran's hand, and he tried to smile back, but he found he was not completely capable of emotion just yet.

They were standing outside the crematorium, where people were waiting for cars to collect them and take them to the wake.

'Would you like to ride with us?' said Ashley.

'If there's room. Yes please.'

Ashley's father Brian drove the car and Kieran sat in the rear seat with Ashley. Kieran didn't know where her mother was, she hadn't attended the funeral.

The car was silent for part of the way, but it was Kieran who spoke first.

'Diane told me you found him.'

Ashley glanced at Kieran and then back out the window at the passing trees, 'Yes I did.'

'That must have been very hard.'

She looked back at him, 'Yes it was. He had this look in his eyes. This vacant look. Indescribable.'

'And you were living with him all that time. Wasn't there any...'

'Any sign? That's a question that just about everyone has managed to ask me. No I don't think I saw any signs that he had this in him, or even that it was imminent. It's not really a thing that I do. Look for signs in people that they might be suicidal.'

'Of course.'

'There were no signs Kieran. The poor thing had something going on in that head of his, and he didn't let any of it show. That's probably why he did it. I mean; he was bottling something up, not sharing it. The pressure must've just... pushed him too far.'

Kieran stared at Ashley, unsure whether to say anything more or let her continue. He remained silent.

'I've had police and psychiatrists over the last ten days tell me that there was a likelihood that Phillip would keep his most treasured secrets away from those who were closest to him. Fair enough, we're probably not supposed to share everything. I mean, yes, I have secrets that I never told him about, but...' She shook her head, 'I don't know. My mind has been twisted in circles this week.'

When Kieran looked at Ashley, he thought he saw all the things that Phillip would have loved about her. He could feel her honesty and her desire to rationalise. It was those grounded qualities that Phillip would have gone for. He would have had such a happy life with her.

So why? Why on Earth did he cut that life short?

~

Kieran stood in the middle of the lounge he had played in so many times as a child. Phillip's childhood home. The home of Diane and Andrew Hynes. The decorations had changed now, yes. But the shape and size were the same, and that was all that was required for Kieran to hear the playful sounds of his youth resonate inside his head.

Looking down at the floor he could see – in his mind - the Scalectrix track he and Phillip had built one Sunday afternoon in that very room some twelve years before. He could almost feel the carpet burns on his knees from kneeling at the side of the track for hours on end, holding the plastic trigger that fired the cars into motion.

The races they used to have. Kieran felt a thin smile find its way to his lips.

'I brought you some food.'

He snapped out of his trance. Ashley was standing next to him holding a plate of assorted corner-cut sandwiches. Kieran took the plate, 'Thank you.'

'I'm struggling a bit here,' Ashley said. 'I'm finding it absolutely stifling being with these people right now. They're all full of concern, wanting to know if I'm okay, and all I want to do is get blind drunk and forget who I am for awhile. I can't... deal with Phillip's family right now. I simply can't.'

Kieran nodded; his mouth was full of sandwich.

'I have to agree,' he said finally. 'Being in this room brings back too many memories that I'd rather forget right now. Phillip and I played in here often.'

'Do you fancy heading back to Ealing and getting a drink. I just want to get shit-faced.'

Kieran hesitated, 'Shouldn't we at least stay a bit longer?'

Ashley shook her head, 'No one's going to make us. They all tread on eggshells around me at the moment. Come on, I'll call us a cab.'

~

The taxi took them to Northfields where they found a bar called Jacksons, which was fashioned out of an old bank, with majestic pillars propping up a high ceiling. The bar was practically empty. It was only five o'clock, and people hadn't finished work yet. Kieran guessed that it would fill up fairly soon.

'I work in a music studio round the back of Wardour Street.' Ashley was saying. 'I'm a desk engineer, so I'm always on hand to help out the producers while they're recording. My usual shifts are twenty-four hours on, twenty-four hours off.'

'That must be pretty tiring. I don't know if I could work those hours.'

'You get used to it. There's plenty of opportunities to find a quiet corner and get some sleep, as there are lots of rest areas with these huge great sofas, and cable TV's, DVD players, stereos, Playstations.'

Ashley adjusted her glasses on her nose and took a sip of her vodka and cranberry juice. Kieran took a sip of his beer.

She continued, 'I left the studio at about a quarter to four in the morning. I got a cab to collect me from the office. The night buses are useless and there's no way I'm wandering the streets at that time of night or sitting at a bus stop shivering my arse off.'

'It's been a very cold October.'

'Yeah, it has. Anyway, I got home at about four-thirty. I was expecting to just clamber into bed next to him, and spend an hour listening to his dreadful snoring before I eventually dropped off to sleep myself. But... but he wasn't in bed. He was in the living room, slumped on the sofa with a bottle of beer in his hand. The television and all the lights were on and I thought he'd just fallen asleep. I tried to wake him, but as I touched his face and felt how cold it was I also realised that his skin was so pale and grey. And his eyes. It was terrifying. Then I saw the sick. He'd vomited on the sofa and all down his front and I hadn't seen it at first. But as soon as I saw the stains I could suddenly smell it. I knew straight away that something was really, really wrong. I checked for his pulse and I found nothing and it... it was horrible. I dropped his arm in disgust. I'm so angry with myself for having that reaction. I ran into the kitchen to call an ambulance. That was when I saw the bottle of cleaning fluid on the sideboard. Looking at how much was left... he could have had as much as half a bottle of the bloody stuff. Well, that's what the post-mortem concluded. He'd masked the taste with the beer.'

As Kieran was visualising the scene, the door to the bar opened a group of four young men in suits came in, making a lot of excited noise, clearly happy to be away from work at the start of the weekend. It disturbed both their thoughts and Ashley seemed to snap out of a trance and look around the room.

'I'm not going too fast am I?'

'No, not at all.'

'Okay,' she continued. 'By then I was pretty much hyperventilating and the woman on the other end of the phone was telling me to calm down so she could take down my details. I told them Phillip had drunk half a bottle of cleaning fluid and he was cold as an iceberg and I really thought he was dead, and that they'd better send an ambulance. Then I called his parents. I let their phone ring and ring until they answered it. I spoke to Andrew and I told him everything. I was crying so hard then that I'm surprised he could even understand what I was saying. They came straight over, just in time to see the paramedic pronounce him dead.'

Kieran could feel tension in his muscles. 'But why would he do that to himself?'

'I've been battling with that question for ten days now and I hate the fact that if I'm no closer to an answer now, then I probably never will be.'

'And there was no note, or journal? Nothing at all?'

Ashley shook her head, 'Like I said. Nothing.'

Kieran was silent awhile. Ashley was watching him, and he was thinking the worst. 'And there's no chance that it could have been...'

She was shaking her head. 'Murder? No, the police never suspected anything like that. There was no evidence to support it. They told me not to touch him so that a forensics team could check for evidence of... of foul play. They dusted for fingerprints, but all they found were his and mine. And fortunately I had an alibi that placed me at the studio at the time of death, which they said was about five or six hours earlier. A few hours later they took his body away. It was horrible. I've never felt so terribly... empty... like that in my whole life.'

'Was there a post mortem?'

'They found a substantial amount of cleaning fluid in his system. He'd taken it with a beer, presumably to block the taste. The inquest is weeks away but the coroner released his body just two days ago.'

They were both silent in thought after that. Kieran was thinking of other questions to ask, but it seemed as though Ashley had filled in all the gaps already.

SPIRECLAW

He looked out through the windows at the cars going by. It was raining hard now. A fine mist of spray was hovering just above the pavement from the impact of a million droplets. Some people had been caught out without umbrellas, and they were running for shelter, holding briefcases and newspapers over their heads for what little relief from the deluge they could get.

'So what will you do now?' Kieran eventually said.

'In a few weeks Diane and Andrew are going to put the house on the market. It's Phillip's house anyway so I won't be living there anymore. It's too intense anyway. Right now I'm staying with my parents.'

'Do you fancy another drink?' said Kieran.

Ashley nodded.

It was the start of a long evening's drinking.

~

Kieran returned from the toilet to find Ashley being chatted up by a guy in a suit who looked only a little more drunk than she was. As he walked across the room back to their table he looked up at the clock above the huge ornate mirror that adorned the rear of the bar. Quarter to eleven. Last orders in fifteen minutes.

'Thanks a lot for the offer,' Ashley was saying to the opportunistic gentleman, 'but my husband wouldn't be too pleased with that.'

Kieran felt a chill run down his spine. He realised they were both looking at him, and Ashley was giggling. The guy had a look on his face that said he'd been the butt of a joke, and he didn't seem to like it. He walked away, through the crowd back to his mates.

Kieran sat down, 'Why did you say that?'

Ashley was still giggling, 'I had to get rid of him somehow.'

Kieran stared at her. He was drunk, but he wasn't having trouble understanding how surreal this evening had been. Here he was, sitting in a bar with the girlfriend of his dead school-buddy, and she was giggling away, as though dismissing the fact that a couple of weeks ago Phillip was alive and well and everything was right with the world.

Ashley's face changed, 'Is something wrong?'

Kieran put his head in his hands. He was starting to feel sick, 'I think I've had too much to drink. This whole thing is a bit too strange. I'm not really sure how I'm supposed to be feeling right now. And, well...'

'And you don't like seeing me laughing,' said Ashley.

'It's not that, it's just. Well, okay. I've really enjoyed this evening. Sitting here chatting with you, getting to know you better. It feels strange though, because we never met before, but we have a common friend. I guess I feel guilty sitting here with you, having a good time, when Phillip's just, just a pile of bloody... ashes. And he's the reason we know each other. Doesn't that feel odd to you?'

Ashley fixed him with a stare he couldn't read; 'I am *not* going to allow anyone to prevent me from disconnecting myself for a few hours.' She stood and gathered her coat off the back of her chair. 'After the week I've had. No sir. No bloody way.'

Kieran stood. 'I'm sorry Ashley. I don't want to spoil anything. Please stay. I'm really sorry.'

She was biting her lip, fighting back tears and staring out of the window at the rain. It had eased off into a light drizzle now.

'Besides,' Kieran continued, 'there's something I want to ask you.'

She looked at him, and at that moment it felt to Kieran like there was nobody else in the bar, despite the noise and the music.

'What?'

'Well, you work in a music studio. Given your experience and expertise; I was wondering if you might know how to fix a broken audiocassette.'

Ashley blinked in surprise, like the question had come out of leftfield. It was obvious that he was attempting to divert the conversation to more stable ground. Then she let out a sigh, and Kieran could see her taught anger turn into weak resignation. He felt relief at seeing her shoulders slump. 'Broken in what way?'

'Well, the tape snapped at the leader. You see, it doesn't belong to me and I need to get it back to its owner. Would you know how to fix it?'

'I don't, but if you give it to me I could get one of the tape guys to look at it at the studio.'

Kieran looked at his watch, 'I have it back at my flat. It's a couple of roads away. Maybe we could go and get it now?'

Ashley looked at her watch. 'Okay, can I call a cab home from your place then?'

'Sure.'

~

Kieran's flat was nice and warm. As he and Ashley stepped through the door, out of the rainy cold, the heat started to thaw his bones.

Gandalf bounced down the hallway to meet them, 'Hello buddy. That's Gandalf.'

Ashley crouched and stroked Gandalf while Kieran switched on the lights. Gandalf miaowed and rubbed his face against Ashley's arm, getting wet from the glistening drops of water that were on her dark coat.

'Careful,' said Kieran as he made his way through to the kitchen, 'He'll eat you.'

'Really? Why?'

'He's a walking bloody waste-disposal unit. He always wants food, and he has a taste for the bizarre.'

'Bizarre?' Ashley stood and followed him down to the kitchen. 'This is a nice place. Do you rent?'

'Yes. Oh... he eats weird stuff. Curry. Mange-tout. His favourite is pizza.'

'Pizza?'

Kieran was filling the kettle from the tap. 'Whenever I order a pizza he always has to have one too. Just a small Meat Feast or something. Thin and crispy. I have to cut it up for him though. Then we watch a movie.'

Ashley laughed. 'Seriously?'

Kieran nodded, smiling, 'Absolutely. Want a coffee?'

'That'd be lovely.' Ashley walked over to the kitchen table and touched the old newspaper, 'What's this?'

Kieran looked round as he took a couple of mugs out of the cupboard. 'What? Oh that. It's just some research I'm doing into something.'

She was looking at the corner of the page. 'Kieran this is really old. It's from the war!'

Kieran opened a can of Whiskas for Gandalf and spooned it into his bowl. 'Yeah, I found it at work I thought it would be interesting to have a read.'

Ashley saw the tape and picked it up. 'Is this the cassette?' She looked closely at the spools.

'That's the one. Reckon it's fixable?'

'Probably.'

Once Kieran had made two coffees he telephoned for a cab.

He was told it would be there in ten minutes. He went and stood next to Ashley. She was swaying on her feet, looking down at the newspaper.

'Cab'll be ten minutes,' he said.

She looked at Kieran. Her eyes were wide. 'I think I've had too much to drink.'

Kieran nodded. 'Me too.'

She stared at him, his nose, his mouth and his neck. He was acutely aware of her wandering eyes examining him.

'Ashley. Erm...does the word "Spireclaw" mean anything to you?' Kieran said.

'The what? Spar-what?'

'Spireclaw.' He spelled it aloud.

Ashley started laughing, some spittle landed on Kieran's face but he didn't wipe it off. She sipped her coffee. 'Nope. Have you looked in the dictionary?'

'I've already tried the dictionary.'

She flipped the newspaper over to show the front page. 'So what is this research you're doing?'

Kieran smiled; he didn't really feel like being drawn into this conversation. Not right now. Not when they'd been drinking for nearly six hours. Not on the day of Phillip's funeral. No. Too many things were going on in his mind.

'Ashley, I promise I will tell you all about it someday. But I think now isn't the time.'

'Why?' she was wearing a playful grin on her face. 'Is it secret?'

'No. It's not secret. Just a little confusing. And possibly a little silly, so I'd really rather talk about it another time.'

Ashley eyed him for a moment, with a look that showed she was trying to see through Kieran, intent on discovering something valuable and special behind his eyes. He stared her down, and eventually she nodded a resignation and raised her finger in front of his face.

'You're a dark horse Kieran Whyteleafe. Phillip told me lots about you,' she turned, almost losing her balance and spilling her coffee in the process. 'But he never told me you had a mysterious side.'

Kieran's smile widened, 'Ah! That's because my mysterious side was so mysterious that even he was unaware of it!'

Ashley was laughing again, but her laugh had begun before he had finished his punchline, so Kieran was left with the awkward feeling that she was laughing *at* him rather than with him.

She took a sip of coffee and dropped the mug a little heavily onto the table. 'They're probably wondering what the hell happened to me. I bet they think I've been consumed by grief and jumped off a bridge or something.'

There was a knock on the front door. The cab had arrived. Within a minute she was gone and the flat was silent.

It was an abrupt and disappointing ending to a crazy evening.

7

I am standing in a hut in Camp II. It is cold in here. Damp and musty smelling. Before me is a thin man, impeccably dressed in a white military coat. He has brown hair hidden under an SS cap. He tells me his name is Captain Stangl, and that he is the Kommandant.

He looks at me disdainfully.
'What is your name?'
'It is Avraham sir,' *I reply.*
'Avraham. I want you to know that my authority here is unquestioned,' he says. 'I have the power of life and death in this camp.'

He motions for me to sit in a chair by a table. I do so, and he takes a seat opposite.

'So you are a goldsmith. Do you have any gold with you?' *he asks.*
'Yes, a little.' *I reply.*
'And your tools. Are they in the bag?'
I nod.
'Show me them.'

I knew he was testing me. A Jew would say he had a skill so that his life might be spared.

I open my bag and remove my tools. A small kerosene burner with a wick, a glass tube, some wire and chisels, and a piece of charcoal.

'Tell me,' said the Kommandant. 'I want to know. How do you make things with these tools?'
'Sir, I heat the charcoal with this burner and I blow on it until it glows. Then I place the hard gold in a hole in the centre of the charcoal. When it melts, I pour the gold into a mold, which I have made with wire. I use the chisel to make the final shape. Sometimes I put lime on my hands to protect it from the heat, but I am so used to the high temperatures that I can work without.'
'Good, good. I want you to make me two rings. One for myself and one for Captain Wagner. How long will you need?'
'I can make them for you in a day.'
'Excellent,' *he stands.*
'Herr Kommandant?'
'Yes?'
'I was wondering about my wife. Her name is Henya,' *I say.* 'She was taken to Camp III yesterday. When might I be able to see her?'

The Kommandant averts my gaze and rubs at a piece of dirt on his hands. 'Soon,' he says. 'She is happy and well, and *enjoying her work in the fields. She is lucky. The work there is easy. You will join her soon.'*

8

The following morning Kieran woke to the driest mouth and sorest head he'd had in months.

It was Saturday, and outside, the weather was being fickle. Yesterday's wind and rain had gone, leaving a virtually cloudless sky. The sun cut through the morning, banishing shadows to some other dark place.

Kieran stood in the kitchen, sipping a strong cup of coffee and staring out at the garden. He could only vaguely remember the slightly surreal night he'd had with Ashley the night before, and he was more than a little confused about her manner. She had been so forward, and because Kieran had never met her before, he was unsure whether she was like that all the time, or whether it was the drink, or even whether it was just an over-compensation for the tragedy of the situation. Either way, he felt wrong-footed.

His thoughts were disturbed by the sound of Gandalf pushing open the cat flap with his head. The cat seemed to be checking the mood of the place before committing himself to entering. He saw Kieran and made the decision to come in. Kieran had pre-empted his arrival and had already filled the cat bowl with food.

Kieran rubbed his temples; he was waiting for the paracetamol to take effect; though with a hangover like this he wondered if the two pills he had taken would be enough.

The letterbox in the front door rattled, and Kieran heard a few envelopes flap to the carpet. Carrying his coffee with him he went to collect them. A bank statement, an AOL CD and an electoral register form. He opened the letters on the way back to the kitchen and dropped them on the table next to the newspaper. Gandalf had finished eating and was staring blankly at him.

He began to think about the day. Saturday morning was a bad time to go to Sainsbury's. It was always so busy, and overrun with screaming mischievous kids, but it was the only time he was able to go, as he never got back in time to go shopping in the evenings. So, despite the fact that his head was booming with the pain of last night's alcohol, he knew he had to just do it. He finished his coffee and put the mug down on the table next to the letters.

That was when he noticed the bank statement he had just opened. Something was wrong with it.

In amongst the cashpoint withdrawals of twenty pounds here, and thirty pounds there, and the council tax direct debit and the phone bill, was a payment of fifty pounds made by cheque. It was a payment he didn't recognise, and Kieran struggled to think of whom he might have written it out to.

The cheque number was 10149.

After mulling it over for a few seconds - during which time he considered that someone might have torn out a cheque from the book while he wasn't looking - he picked up the telephone and dialed the number for his bank. A recorded message told him that his branch was closed, and that he needed to call back during business hours, which meant he would have to wait until Monday.

He replaced the receiver and went to get his workbag from the living room. From it, he took out his chequebook and flipped through the stubs to cheque 10149.

The stub was blank. Kieran was taken aback. He always filled in the stubs. At least he thought he did.

Looking at the bank statement, Kieran saw that the cheque was paid in a week ago, though the cheque would obviously have been written sometime before. The two stubs on either side of the blank stub were a week apart, and that was three weeks ago. Try as he might, he couldn't remember what he'd written the cheque out for.

The solution to that particular puzzle would just have to wait until Monday.

~

SPIRECLAW

As the morning gave way to afternoon, the clear skies gave way to dark ominous clouds, and a hard driving rain fell out of the sky. Kieran sat with Gandalf on the living room couch eating carrot cake and drinking tea, enjoying the cosiness of being shut in with his cat for the rest of the afternoon while the rain hammered down outside.

There was show jumping on the television, but Kieran wasn't watching it. He was thinking about Spireclaw. Whenever he brought the word to the front of his mind, dusted it down and re-examined it, he felt as though it was pushing at the edge of his senses, elusively trying to get away. The dictionary had declared the word as unknowable, which meant it was little more than a jumble of letters. And what were letters without meaning? In fact, when he thought about it, the only reason he had devoted this much grey matter to it was because he'd seen the word written twice, in two far removed locations in space and time.

The telephone rang. It startled both Kieran and Gandalf. The cat was clearly put out by such a rude interruption and he leapt off the sofa. Kieran got up and went into the kitchen to answer the shrill ring.

'Hello?'

'Kieran hi, it's Ashley.'

'Oh hi. How are you feeling?' Out of the back window Kieran could see a torrent of water toppling from the gutter that ran along the back of the house and splashing into the drain on the patio. The wind had knocked over some empty plant pots. It was a thoroughly miserable day outside.

'Please, don't ask. I feel like someone's driven a truck over my skull.'

'Oh, nice.'

'This weather doesn't help my state of mind either.'

'I know what you mean.'

There was a slightly awkward pause, then Ashley said, 'I've just got into work, though I'd much rather be in bed sleeping off this hangover.'

'I can imagine.'

'But, well I brought that tape in with me to give to one of the guys here to fix and, well, it's not broken.'

'Not broken? What do you...?'

'Look. Honestly Kieran. We're you playing a joke on me or something?'

'A joke? Of course not. What do you mean it's not broken? You saw it last night. The tape had snapped at the leader.'

'Well,' Ashley said. 'That's what I thought I saw. In all honesty I was so bloody drunk, I wouldn't have been surprised if... if your cat had struck up a conversation with me.'

'I promise you Ashley. I'm not the sort of guy who plays practical jokes. Especially under the circumstances.'

He waited for her to acknowledge his honesty, but she remained silent.

'So you listened to the tape?' he added.

'Yes, I did. It's a bit weird though. I can't imagine why it's so important to you. Did you make the recording?'

'No.' Kieran said. He was wondering how he was going to explain that he'd actually stolen it from his office. Well, borrowed rather. But would she even care?

'Is it something to do with that newspaper?' she said.

Kieran wasn't sure how to answer. 'I don't know. Well, theoretically, yes.'

'Theoretically?'

Kieran thought maybe he shouldn't tell her any more than he already had. He realised that this was where he decided if he wanted it to be his own thing or not. His instinct was telling him to keep it to himself. But hadn't he already involved her by asking for her help with the tape? But then, hadn't that been just to say something to change the subject when he thought he'd offended her the night before? And was it even something that merited the time and attention he was giving it?

'Ashley, look. Could you make a copy of the tape?'

'Sure.'

'And are you free tomorrow night?'

'Tomorrow night?'

'We could get a meal somewhere.'

There was a brief pause on the line.

'I've got some things I need to sort out.'

'Monday then.'

'I'm working Monday night. But I can do Tuesday,' she said.

Kieran noticed Gandalf sitting near his empty bowl staring accusingly up at him, 'Tuesday it is then. I'll tell you about the tape and the newspaper over dinner.'

9

It was the last Monday in October. A solid grey fog had folded itself around the roofs of all the houses, stealing the chimney tops and smearing vaseline on the streetlamps, so that each light was adorned with an angelic halo.

It was cold outside, and not the sort of day for Kieran to be standing on a freezing tube platform, waiting for the Piccadilly Line train to take him into town.

While he waited, his mind returned to Ashley.

After one drunken evening, a phone call and a favour, Kieran felt very comfortable with her. Her forward manner made him warm to her. He found he wanted to tell her all about Spireclaw. To him it was a way of connecting his past with Phillip to the present with Ashley. And because she and Phillip had been an item, she might just like to hear something new about him. But then again, perhaps that was the last thing she wanted.

At work, during the mid morning rush between the first and second mail round, while Mr Cray was in a meeting, Kieran used the telephone on Cray's desk to call his bank.

He was connected to a young woman with a Glasweigian accent. He told her his name and account number.

'Good morning Mr Whyteleafe. Could you please tell me the fourth digit of your security number?'

'Erm. Seven.'

'And the ninth digit please.'

'Three.'

'Thank you Mr Whyteleafe. How can I help you today?'

'I wanted to find out the name of the payee on a cheque that was cashed a week ago. Cheque number 10149. I forgot to write the name on the stub.'

'Just one minute sir.'

Kieran heard her tapping away on a distant keyboard. A pause, followed by more tapping.

'Hello sir?'

'Yes?'

'The cheque was made out to a Mr David Everett.'

'David Everett, thank you. And do you have an address for him?'

'I'm sorry we don't,' said the woman. 'Our instruction is just to transfer the funds over to his account, and as he is with a different bank, we don't hold any of his details.'

'I see,' Kieran was writing "David Everett" on a Post-it note. 'Well thank you very much for your help.'

'Is there anything else I can help you with today Mr Whyteleafe?'

'No, thank you.'

'Okay then, goodbye.'

'Goodbye.'

Kieran replaced the receiver.

He looked at the name he had written on the page. David Everett. He had never come across it before. So why had he written a cheque for fifty pounds out to the man?

Kieran contemplated picking up the phone and calling his bank again. It may have been too late to stop the cheque, but he could still report fraud.

He checked himself, deciding that he might do a little investigation himself first.

~

There is an unwritten rule among the initiated that states you always need something two weeks after you throw it away, and that the time is reduced if you owned the thing for longer in the first place. The same applies to bulk storage. It was very likely, Kieran thought, that Edward Gosnell would need to gain access to his boxes straight away, as was often the case.

SPIRECLAW

But if the boxes went a full two weeks without him calling them back, then it was likely that they would never be needed again. Kieran wanted to make sure.

That afternoon, in the lull after the lunch hour, before the first of the afternoon mail rounds, Kieran went down to the sub-basement to look at cage 14. He was relieved to find that the boxes were arranged just as he'd left them. Clearly Edward Gosnell hadn't put in a request for them, and if Kieran wanted to, he could probably steal the boxes and nobody would ever know.

~

That evening, after Kieran and Gandalf were fully fed, and the latest events in Albert Square had unfolded on the television, Kieran took out the local phone book from the small shelf by the front door and skipped through it to the letter E.

There were two entries for Everett, D.

Kieran wondered which name, if either, was the one he'd paid fifty pounds to.

He picked up phone in the kitchen and dialed the number of the first entry.

A young woman answered the phone, 'Hello?'

'Hello. Could I please speak with David Everett?'

There was a pause on the line, 'I'm sorry, who?'

'D. Everett?'

'There's no David Everett here.'

'Then I'm sorry to have bothered you, said Kieran. 'I must have the wrong number.'

He put the phone down and dialed the second number. It was answered before Kieran's phone registered that it had even rung.

'Hello?' said a man, who seemed put out that his phone had rung.

'Hello. Is this David Everett?'

'Yes this is he.'

Kieran felt the blood drain out of his face. All of a sudden he had no idea what to say. He contemplated hanging up the receiver. Perhaps this wasn't the right David Everett anyway.

'What do you want?' the man said.

'I'm sorry to bother you. My name is Kieran Whyteleafe, and...'

'Oh, hello Kieran. I didn't recognise your voice for a second there.'

Kieran pulled his head away from the phone. *What?*

The man spoke again, 'Did you get the boxes alright?'

Kieran was trying to blink away the confusion. His brain was trying to piece it together.

'Boxes?' Kieran said, his voice had broken down into a half whisper.

'Yes. I sent them to your office like you asked,' said David.

Kieran was at a complete loss for what to say. He started to feel sick. His mouth went dry. His eyes darted around the kitchen, hunting for some sense in the situation. He found himself looking at the phone book. Specifically at the address of the man he was talking to.

Number 7, Highfield Road, Ealing.

A shiver ran down his entire body.

7 Highfield Road was the address of his childhood home. The house he and his mother had lived in when he was a child. The house where he and Phillip had seen the word "Spireclaw" written in that dark cellar all those years ago.

'I'm sorry,' Kieran said. 'I don't know what you're talking about.'

David Everett said nothing for a few seconds. Then, 'Are you alright mate?'

'I think I must be going mad...'

10

Kieran felt guilty to think it, but when he saw Ashley approach his table near the window at the restaurant, she looked quite beautiful. It was Tuesday night, the night after Kieran had put in a call to David Everett, and they had arranged to meet at Jalsha in Ealing Broadway for a curry.

Kieran had arrived a little early, so he was already sipping a beer when she arrived.

There was something about the light that made her face look radiant, and when the waiter took her coat and scarf Kieran was literally stunned by how sexy she looked in her little black strappy dress.

Wasn't it a little cold to be wearing something like that?

Only now was he fully seeing her, and he realised just how dreamlike last Friday had been. He hated himself for acknowledging that she was attractive, as though he was somehow betraying Phillip for having such unclean thoughts.

Her hair was dark brown, long and straight, but it always seemed to rest on her shoulders in a different way, framing her face uniquely each time. Sometimes she tucked it behind her ears, only to have it fall back in front of her eyes. He liked that.

She was a slim girl, and not very tall, and to Kieran she was shaped just right.

Apart from the two of them and the waiters, the restaurant was empty.

'Sorry I'm late,' she said.

'You're not late. I was early.'

Ashley put the two audiocassettes on the table and sat down, 'I made a copy like you asked.'

'Oh, thank you.' He picked up the cassettes. 'How much do I owe you?'

She waved her hand dismissively. 'Don't worry. Blank tapes are cheap as chips.'

The waiter arrived and handed them each a menu. She asked if she could have a glass of red wine.

'I'm amazed that it was fixed when you looked at it,' said Kieran. 'It really was totally broken when I gave it to you.'

He opened the original cassette box and took out the cassette. He examined it for moment and then put his finger in the spool to see that it had tension. It did.

'Well I'm flabbergasted! I really am. I don't understand how it can have done this all by itself.'

Ashley smiled. 'I don't understand it either.'

The waiter came back with Ashley's wine and took their orders. Ashley ordered a Prawn Korma and Kieran ordered a Chicken Tikka Masala.

'So what is all this about?' she said.

Kieran was about to speak when the door to the restaurant rattled open. He looked up to see two couples enter. They were taken to a table near the back of the restaurant.

Kieran momentarily searched for a place to begin.

'It's like this. When Phillip and I were thirteen, he came over one night to my house in Highfield Road to stay the night. Our house had a really great cellar underneath it and we went down there to smoke a couple of cigarettes. We sat in the part of the cellar that was underneath my bedroom. I had a ground floor bedroom. I'd laid some blankets down on the concrete and made it reasonably comfortable for us to sit down there. I often sneaked down there for a cigarette.'

The two couples at the back of the restaurant laughed loudly, disturbing Kieran's train of thought. He took a sip of his beer and continued.

'While we were down there, we saw this word that had been written on one of the brick pillars. Spireclaw. Written in white paint. The thing is, I'd never seen it before and I'd sat down there loads of times. Well, Phillip and I had visions of someone sneaking around in the dark with us. It freaked us both out and we didn't stick around much longer. We went back upstairs. And that was that. I gave it no more thought for the last twelve years. Until last Monday. The day Phillip died. I was late for work. I missed my mail-round so my boss asked me to take some archive boxes down to one of the cages in the sub-basement of the building. While I was down there I saw the word again. Spireclaw. It was written in the dust on a window. If it had been any other word I probably wouldn't have cared. But seeing it brought back all those...'

He saw that Ashley had tears in her eyes.

'What's wrong?'

She shook her head. 'You're telling me something about Phillip I never knew. There must be so many things about him I never had the time to discover.' She wiped her eyes and dropped her hands to the table. 'I just miss him.'

SPIRECLAW

Kieran folded his hands around one of hers.

'I know you do,' he said.

'Please continue. I want to hear it all.'

Kieran nodded. 'Okay. Well. A bit later on in the day I tried to call Phillip. Just to say hi and ask him if he remembered that night in the cellar. I kept getting an engaged tone and I eventually called Diane.'

'Yes,' said Ashley. 'The phone was in use for most of the day. There were so many people we had to inform.'

'Diane said it was a coincidence that I called that day. And just thinking about it gives me shivers. All these things seem to be connected. Spireclaw appeared to me on the day of his death. And last time we saw it we were together in the basement. I rang him because I wanted to ask him if he'd ever seen the word elsewhere. Something tells me there's a connection between Spireclaw and Phillip. Something about the timings.'

'So where does the tape come into all this?'

Kieran let out a deep breath. 'This is the part that really scares the hell out of me. I mean it really makes me question my damn sanity. All these disconnected things and how they come together.'

'What do you mean?'

'Okay. The tape was in one of a set of boxes I was asked to take down to the basement at work. So was the newspaper. Well, there were lots of newspapers actually, all dated... erm...October 15th 1943. Anyway, the only reason I went back down to look in those boxes was because the name on the side of them was someone who didn't seem to work at the company. His name was Edward Gosnell, and his name didn't appear in the company phone directory or on the temp list. I thought it might be a security issue, having those boxes sitting down there. Could have been a bomb, and my boss didn't seem to care. So I went down and looked inside. And this is the thing that baffles me more than any of it. The thing that I just plain don't understand. Especially after the telephone conversation I had last night...'

'What telephone conversation?'

'Last night I called this guy on the phone. His name was David Everett. No wait. Hang on, I'd better backtrack a bit. Okay. On Saturday I got my bank statement through the post. There was an entry in it that I didn't recognise. It was a cheque I'd written for fifty quid. But I have absolutely no recollection of ever writing it out. I hadn't even filled in the stub. I called the bank and they told me it was paid to this guy called David Everett. So I looked him up in the phone book, and his address... His bloody address is 7 Highfield Road. My old bloody house.'

Ashley was wide eyed, 'And, what did this David Everett guy say when you called him.'

'He asked if I'd received the boxes okay.'

She put up her hands, 'Whoa. Hold on a minute. The man who lives in your old house was the one who sent the boxes to your office?'

Kieran was smiling, 'Yes. But get this, at my request. Apparently I wrote him a letter, then followed up with a telephone call about two weeks ago. He said I sent him a cheque for fifty pounds and asked him to box up all the newspapers in the cellar and write "Edward Gosnell 14R" on the side of each one and then send them to my work. I don't remember doing that at all. I never wrote to him and I certainly don't remember calling him, or writing a cheque.'

'So you think someone's winding you up?'

'It's got to be. It doesn't make any sense otherwise. I do remember the newspapers though. There really were newspapers in that cellar. I remember seeing them when I was a kid.'

'But what about the tape?'

'The tape. David said I'd told him that the tape was in a plastic Tesco's bag near the newspapers in the cellar. I don't remember the tape though. I don't remember the Tesco's bag. Can you believe they were sitting there all this time?'

Ashley sat back, 'I don't really know what to say.'

Kieran shook his head. 'Is it really possible that I could be doing things without even knowing it? Could I really have made a telephone call, and sent a cheque without remembering?'

Ashley was shaking her head. 'I doubt it.'

'Is there a possibility that I have some kind of... I don't know. A mental disorder?'

'Oh come on Kieran. Look, I think you're mistaken. There must be some logical explanation for all this. I wouldn't be surprised if someone's playing a joke on you. It is Halloween tomorrow after all.'

'Good point. It's a little too elaborate though, don't you think?'

'I don't know how resourceful your friends are.'

'None of my friends would do this. Anyway. Look. I'm going over to see this David Everett guy on Friday. I've asked to see the letter and, well, I was wondering if you would like to come along. I think I might need someone... I think I'd like you... to be with me.'

11

I finish the rings and give them to Kommandant Stangl, he is very pleased and I feel a wave of relief wash over me. He leaves with them clutched tightly in his hand and returns a few minutes later with a bowl of soup and some hot fresh buttered bread for me. I eat the food and it tastes delicious. I am beginning to realise that I can survive here if I am useful to the guards.

The Kommandant drops a handful of rings and bracelets onto the table. Some of them clatter onto the floor.

'I want you to make a nameplate for me, to fit on the door of my hut. Can you do this?'

'Yes sir.' I tell him.

Later that day, the door to my workshop opens. A Blackie walks in. He tells me his name is Klat.

'I have a something for you. I will give it to you if you make a bracelet for my wife.'

'I don't have enough gold to make a bracelet,' I say. 'With the gold I have I am making a nameplate for the Kommandant.'

'I will get you the gold you need.'

'Then I will start on it as soon as I have finished the nameplate.'

'Good.' Klat reaches into his pocket and pulls out a piece of paper. He gives it to me.

It is a letter from Gavrel, my good friend who was taken to Camp III the day we arrived. Tears fill my eyes. I am so glad he is still alive.

'I want the bracelet in three days,' says Klat as he steps out of the workshop.

I quickly read Gavrel's letter.

Dearest Avraham,

I am working in Camp III, and I see every day the inhumanity and atrocity the German guards are committing and I wonder how it is allowed. They are killing us all. They tell the Jews that they are going to work in the fields, and that they will take a shower first. The Jews are ordered to remove their clothes. Then they are locked into a chamber. A hundred at a time. The room is filled with Carbon Monoxide pumped from an engine behind the Camp. The cries and sounds of vomiting are unbearable. It takes ten minutes for them to die. Then the floor of the room drops open, and the bodies fall into carts. My job is to pull the carts out to the fields and bury the bodies.

Sometimes the bodies stir while we bury them, but the guards shoot them.

The trains will continue to come, and more of our brothers and sisters will be killed. This cannot be allowed to go on. Somebody must tell the world about Sobibor. I am sure that our story is missing from every newspaper in the world. I am sure our story is untold.

Tonight you must say the Kaddish for all who died and will continue to die here. Say it for me, as I will never be allowed to walk alive from here. But if there is ever a chance that you can escape from these sadistic Nazis, then take it, because it will be the most important thing you ever do.

Your friend, Gavrel.

Crying hard, I burn the letter. I could not risk being caught with it by any of the SS guards.

12

Walking up Highfield Road in the Autumn dark was like opening a door to a room full of memories Kieran had thought was shut away forever.

Ashley was walking next to him, and she was staring up at the houses, oblivious to the emotional impact this place was having on him. He remembered his old Walkman, and the tape he used to listen to at exactly this time of year - November – walking down this very street when the weather was just like this.

Phil Collins. No Jacket Required. He'd copied the tape off Phillip and someone had pressed the record button halfway through "Only You Know and I Know". He found himself singing the song in his head now as he walked.

Whenever I think I know you better,
Better than I know myself,
Ooh, I open up, and give you everything, then you,
You say "Okay, what else?"

Suddenly the song had a different meaning. It was no longer a dialog between a man and a woman; it was a dialog between Kieran and himself; the Kieran he understood, and the other Kieran, which performed dark acts with some strange purpose.

In the sky, the low, heavy clouds were orange. They were reflecting the streetlights of London, and there was a thin fog and the smell of gunpowder because this was the beginning of the bonfire weekend.

A mild wind was brushing against his face, but it was warm for early November. On the ground the autumn leaves had been flattened to the pavement by rain, making the going a little slippery.

He even recognised the shapes of the kerbstones, as he recalled the times when he used to sit on them eating sweets in the summer holidays when he was young, or kick a football against them until a car came along.

Occasionally the distant sound of a rocket being launched with a whoosh-crackle into the sky followed by a resonant bang drowned out the sound of the swishing wet-tyre traffic on the main road behind them.

In amongst Kieran's nostalgia for this childhood place was nervousness. They were drawing closer to number seven, and Kieran could feel his heart rate increasing with every single step.

They turned onto the property and weaved through the two cars parked on the gravel driveway. Kieran looked up at the house.

It was a 1930's three-storey detached house in red-brown brick, with bay windows on the ground floor and in the first floor master bedroom. The front door was set into the building, creating a porch area under the overhang created by the room above.

Kieran found himself smiling at the shape of the house. He had attained a level of familiarity with it that surpassed any feelings about any other house he lived in. It said something about the difference between the sharpness with which a young mind processes what it sees, and the way that receptiveness is blunted, as the mind gets older.

They were standing in the porch. Ashley rang the doorbell and the man who answered introduced himself as David Everett. He invited them in.

Inside, not only was the decor different but so was the layout. The kitchen had been extended into a conservatory that had eaten up a portion of the garden, and the wall that separated the living room with the main hall had been knocked through, creating a huge arched walk-through.

Seeing the house like this, changed after so many years saddened Kieran. This experience was corrupting his original picture of the house, and would no doubt always creep in to his thoughts when he remembered his younger days here.

David Everett lived here with his wife, who - he told them - was away in New York on business.

They sat in the living room drinking tea, David on one sofa and Ashley and Kieran on the other.

David picked up the letter off the coffee table and handed it to Kieran. He uttered a small nervous laugh. 'Sorry about the soggy bit, I had to fish it out of the bin.'

Kieran looked at the address on the envelope, 'It's my handwriting.' He pulled out the single folded sheet of paper and opened it.

To whom it may concern,
Ten years ago I lived in your house. I had gathered some things in the cellar, which I forgot to remove when we left. I would be most grateful if you would box up the newspapers in the cellar and the contents of the Tesco bag nearby and send them to the mailroom at Arthur Andersen, 1 Surrey Street, London. Please mark each box with "Edward Gosnell 14R". I have enclosed sufficient funds to cover costs.
Yours sincerely,
Kieran Whyteleafe

Kieran passed the letter to Ashley. She took it and started to read. Kieran looked at David. 'I have that type of paper, and those envelopes at home. It's in my hand, and I recognise the ink, it's from the pen in my kitchen. So it's fairly conclusive that I wrote it, but I have no recollection of it at all.'

Ashley put the letter back on the table and said to David; 'What time and date did Kieran telephone you?'

'It was three weeks ago last Tuesday, at about ten in the evening. So that was October 8th, right?'

Ashley looked at Kieran. 'Can you remember that evening?'

Kieran put his head down into his hands and tried to think.

'Tuesday three weeks ago. I think I called my mother in Cape Town.' That was at about 8 o'clock. We talked for about half an hour. Then I watched some television and went to bed. I was in bed asleep before ten.'

The others two were silent.

'Are you saying I'm doing all this in my sleep?'

Ashley turned to David again. 'What did he sound like on the phone? This was after you received the letter right?'

'Yes,' said David. 'He sounded perfectly normal. Just like he does now.'

Kieran said; 'Did you see the word Spireclaw written on one of the brick supports in the cellar? Underneath the ground floor bedroom?'

'No, there's nothing like that down there.' said David.

'Maybe someone removed it in the intervening years,' said Ashley.

Kieran suddenly felt too warm. He could feel himself beginning to sweat. He felt uncomfortable. He didn't want to be there anymore. He couldn't escape the feeling that he was close to discovering a truth that was meant to stay hidden from him. He stood up and offered his hand. 'David. Listen. I'm sure this is all a bit weird for you. I want to thank you for everything.'

David and Ashley stood as well.

David smiled and shook Kieran's hand. 'I'm not really sure what to say about all this.'

'Me neither. I feel like I've got amnesia, but I don't ever remember banging my head.'

'Well if there's anything else I can help you with,' added David. 'Please let me know.'

~

Walking down Highfield Road, away from the house, the smell of burning was much stronger now. Kieran tried to focus his mind on all the facts. But his thoughts were spread too thinly, over too many aspects of the puzzle, and he could conclude nothing. He said. 'I have more questions now than I did when I went in there.'

Ashley tucked her arm under his. 'Fancy a drink?'

SPIRECLAW

They went back to Jacksons. It was a busy night. Friday's were always rammed. The smokey atmosphere was stifling, but the jolly sounds of a hundred people chatting and laughing comforted Kieran.

'I feel like I've gone full circle,' he said. 'After all this hunting around I've ended up right back where I started. I don't know where to look to find the answers. Perhaps I should see a doctor. If I'm really doing things without knowing. Well I could cause myself an injury. Wander in front of a car or something.'

Ashley was shaking her head, and running her index finger around the rim of her wine glass. 'You haven't gone round in circles. You haven't ended up where you started, because all roads lead to Edward Gosnell. You asked for his name to be written on those boxes. Somewhere in that brain of yours is the answer to who Edward Gosnell really is. It's time you found out.'

'You're right,' said Kieran. He realised that in his anxiety he had pulled a strip of skin away from the cuticle on his thumb.

'Kieran. Can I stay at your place tonight?'

An absolutely leftfield question. Kieran looked directly at her. 'Ashley, I...'

'It's just, I don't like going back to my parents house. They treat me like some precious diamond or something. I'll sleep on the sofa. Just give me a blanket and I'll be fine.'

'No. I'll sleep on the sofa. You can have my bed.'

'There's another reason too.'

'Really? What?'

'There's something else I want to ask you. Something that I've been thinking about since Phillip died.'

'What's that?' Kieran's heart began to pump a little harder, was she beginning to feel an attraction towards him? Was she about to suggest something that would make his night?

Ashley lowered her head and looked at the table. 'I was wondering. Have you ever done a seánce?'

~

Ashley was cutting a sheet of paper into small pieces. Each piece had a letter or number on it, which she had written with a black marker pen.

'You have to arrange the letters and numbers in a circle, and the words YES and NO at opposite ends.'

Soon she had them all arranged like she said and was signaling for him to place his index finger on the upturned glass that she had placed in the centre of the circle, just like she had.

Kieran's hand quivered over the glass, and then he retracted it and shook his head. 'I must admit I'm more than a bit scared.'

'I don't think there's anything to worry about. Besides, I can't do it on my own. For some reason it needs at least two of us.'

'How many times have you done this before?'

'A few.'

'And does it actually work?'

'Yes. Pretty much every time.'

They were both sitting cross-legged on the floor on either side of the low coffee table in Kieran's living room. At the edge of the table was a newly opened bottle of Cabernet Sauvignon and two freshly filled wine glasses.

Ashley had lit some candles "for effect" and had placed them on the floor surrounding the table.

Kieran placed his finger on the glass.

They waited in silence. Out of the corner of his eye Kieran saw Gandalf appear at the door to the living room. He rubbed his nose against the jamb.

'Gandalf,' said Kieran quietly. 'You can come in here if you like but for God's sake stay away from the candles.'

Ashley giggled. 'Come on this is serious!'

Gandalf performed a u-turn and wandered slowly off towards the kitchen.

Kieran looked at the glass again, and almost straight away it began to move, slowly at first, as though it would be berated for such an act, but then just a little quicker.

'Is there anybody there?' Ashley whispered. Ashley's eyes were fixed on Kieran, rather than the glass.

SPIRECLAW

The glass began a movement towards the piece of paper marked YES.

'Jeeesus,' whispered Kieran 'Are you doing that?'

Ashley ignored him. 'What is your name?'

The glass started to slide in the opposite direction.

ROW

'Write it down!' whispered Ashley.

Kieran wrote the letters on a notepad he had balancing on his knee.

Then it spelled the word KIERAN

'Is that you Phillip?' said Ashley.

There was a pause. In the still quiet of the flat, Ashley's stomach rumbled loudly, and normally Kieran would probably have laughed. But all forms of humour were suddenly far from his mind just then.

NO

'Can you tell us about Phillip?'

DEAD

'Are you dead?' said Kieran.

NO

'Then what are you?'

ROW

Ashley took her finger off the glass and shook her arm. Kieran's arm was aching too. He also took his away.

'What does ROW mean, do you suppose?' said Ashley.'

Kieran shrugged and sipped his wine 'Beats me. I don't know what ROW means. But I'm okay to carry on for a bit longer if you are,' he said. 'This is definitely the weirdest thing I've ever done.'

Ashley took a sip of her wine and laid her finger on the glass, 'Come on.'

The glass was quick to move again after they resumed, as though it was now eager to tell them something, even though it had previously been hesitant.

3OMAL

'I'm thinking this is a waste of time.' said Kieran, writing down the letters as they appeared. 'None of this makes much sense.'

ROWNPA

'Does this make any sense to you?' he added.'

SSAG

'Wait,' said Kieran to the glass, or to whatever was controlling it. 'Stop for a minute. Please can you start again?'

Outside the windows the wind blew up into a gust and stirred the trees, a few droplets of rain appeared on the window, creating a hundred warped reflections of the orange streetlamps outside.

CROWNPASSAGE

Kieran felt a shiver manipulate his spine, and it was definitely a shiver created by fear and wonder. Ashley uttered a nervous laugh. 'Oh my God, it's actually telling us to go somewhere.'

'Do you think so?'

'Well of course it is?'

'Crown Passage. Do you even know where that is?'

'No, do you?'

Kieran stared out of the window at the night, 'No.'

'Sounds like it's in London, though. London has lots of passages. Have you got an A to Z?'

Kieran stood up, his knees clicking loudly, 'Ooh me legs! I've got one in my bag.' He went out into the hall and pulled the little book out of his workbag.

He was already flipping through the index. 'This book only covers the centre of town though. Crown Passage, Crown Passage, Crown Passage. Ah, here we are. Crown Passage. There's one in SW1. B-Six, forty-three. B-Six, forty-three.'

Kieran flicked to page forty-three and found square B6. 'It's near St James's Street.'

'Off Piccadilly,' said Ashley.

'Sort of. Actually it's nearer Pall Mall.' He handed her the book, with his thumb on Crown Passage. She took it and looked more closely.

Kieran picked up the notepad, on which he had written everything that had been spelled out so far. 'So do you think 30MAL means number thirty Pall Mall?'

She looked up from the A to Z. 'Might do I suppose.'

They were silent. Kieran could hear Gandalf scratching his claws on the wicker washing basket in the kitchen.

'STOP THAT GANDALF.'
Gandalf stopped.
Ashley said, 'Do you think we should carry on?'
'Yes.'
They placed their fingers on the upturned glass and waited.
And they waited.
But the glass didn't move.

13

I hear the sound of glass smashing and it shocks me out of concentration. I look up from my work. There is shouting outside. I position myself so that I can look out of the hut and see what is happening.

Two Jews have been carrying a pane of glass. A window. It lies in pieces on the ground. Shattered after they dropped it. A guard is whipping one of the Jews, forcing him to the ground.

'You idiot,' the guard shouts. He bends to the ground and picks up a small piece of glass, and another. He pushes them into the Jew's mouth. 'Eat it you fool.'

While the Jew is eating the glass, blood is pouring out of his cheek through a hole cut from the inside.

The guard takes his pistol and shoots the Jew in the head. He slumps to the floor.

Barry, the dog that belongs to the guards, is ordered to bite the leg of the other Jew.

I think about Gavrel's letter. I realise now more than ever that I must escape.

I see the Kommandant approach from a hut on the other side of the Camp, he steps around the dead Jew like he is avoiding a piece of rubbish. He reaches the steps of my workshop but before he climbs them he looks down at his uniform and flattens his jacket with both of his hands. He has not seen me through the dusty window and now I dare not move in case he sees me. He would punish me for not working I am sure. Fortunately, the door opens inwards as he opens it and steps in I have time to move back into my chair. He comes round the door walks slowly over to my table and sits in the chair opposite.

I want to kill him. This man is responsible for the death of my wife, and he enjoys watching my fellow Jews die.

I want to kill him but I must show no anger in my face. If the Kommandant thinks for even a moment that I know about what happens in Camp III then he will not hesitate to send me there too.

Gavrel risked his life to get me that letter. I need to honour him by escaping and telling the world about Sobibor.

It occurs to me that if I ask the Kommandant about my wife, he may not suspect that I know about the murdering that goes on in Camp III.

'Kommandant. About my wife, Henya. I wonder when I might see her.'

Again he replies, 'Soon. She is enjoying her work in the fields. She said to tell you that she looks forward to seeing you.'

I nod, trying desperately in my heart to keep myself from crying.

'Tomorrow,' says the Kommandant, 'a new train will arrive with more Jewish workers for the fields. I will need you and some of your fellows to clean out the carriages after they are empty. Afterwards you will return to your work here.'

I nod. 'Yes Kommandant.'

The Kommandant reaches into his pocket and pulls out a handful of jewelry. He places them on the table. Scarred gold rings, bracelets and necklaces. Gold teeth. I recognise the heart shaped pendant that I made for my wife. The chain is still broken from where the other guard had torn it from her sweet neck.

'I want you to melt these items and make them into ten rings. One for each of the guards in my immediate command. I will give you their initials. You are to engrave each ring with an initial. If you do this I will be very happy.'

Without hesitation I say yes. But my mind is screaming with torment. Not only is my poor wife dead by their despicable hands, but also now I am forced to destroy her most treasured *possession so that a Nazi can wear it on his finger like a trophy.*

Never. I would sooner die.

After the Kommandant is gone I take my pendant and hide it in my shoe. Later I will hide it somewhere else, and if I ever manage to escape, it will come with me. I will never let it out of my sight.

14

The following morning Ashley is the first to wake. Her eyes flutter open and she is temporarily disorientated; confused about where she is.

She is in Kieran's bed. She has stayed the night.

She listens to the flat. It is quiet. The bedside clock says 8:14am. Kieran must still be asleep in the living room.

A dead weight is pushing the duvet down beside her leg. It is Gandalf. He is staring at her, purring.

'Hello cat,' she says. He half closes his eyes.

Ashley sighs and perches her head on a folded pillow. 'Y'know Gandalf, I'm a confused girly. I really am. Only a few weeks ago I was lying on the bed in the hotel room in Fuerteventura, making love to man who is now dead. The thought sends shivers through me and makes me want to cry. Even now he's not with me I can still hear him speaking.'

Gandalf's ears spin round and his eyes become alert, as though he is hearing a noise.

'Can you hear him, little cat? Do you have a level of perception that goes beyond humans? When your ears turn like that, is that you picking up his voice? If it is, tell him I love him. Oh Gandalf I wish I could talk to him myself.'

Gandalf becomes restful again, and lies his head down on his paws.

'And now Kieran has appeared in my life. Yes, your boss; the hand that feeds you. He has a quality about him that touches something in me. He doesn't pander to my grief. He just treats me normally.'

'I think I have feelings for him beyond just friends. But it's forbidden right? There are unwritten rules about love, and courting the friend of an ex-lover is just about the worst one to break.'

'Oh look at me. I'm sobbing all over his pillow. How could I expect you to understand? You're just a cat. I don't think cats have as much of a problem when it comes to loyalty. Mating is a far more predatory thing when you have four legs, right?'

She strokes his soft fur, 'I think humans can be predatory too.'

~

Kieran woke abruptly. He'd had a bad night sleeping awkwardly on the sofa, and now the lower part of his back was aching.

Gandalf was sitting on his chest with his little cat face just a few inches away from Kieran's.

The flat smelled of sizzling bacon and fresh coffee. The clock on the video said 10am.

Kieran looked at Gandalf.

'D'ya know what cat? I'm struggling to understand that girl. I'm pretty damn confused about how she fits into my life.

'Two weeks ago I didn't even know her. Now I feel like I've known her all my life. It's like we have this powerful connection. It's obviously because of the grief we share, but it seems like more than that, Gandalf. Lots more.'

Gandalf didn't move. Kieran stroked him.

'I know what you're thinking. You think I'm trying to justify my reasons for liking her, and absolve myself at the same time. Absolve myself of the guilty feelings I have because the reality is, she's the girlfriend of my oldest friend Phillip, who was put in the ground just a week ago.

'How could I expect you to understand? You're just a cat. Life for you is a simple oscillation between eating and sleeping. No complexities there, my friend. No tales of love and betrayal were ever told from a cat's point of view. And betrayal is exactly what this is. Even by thinking these thoughts I am betraying Phillip. This is no way to honourably grieve his loss.

SPIRECLAW

And I'm sure there's no room in Ashley's head for anything but Phillip and the things that surrounded him. I'm sure she only pays attention to me because I was part of his life. There was a connection between Phillip and me that she wants to examine, like an electrician wiring a plug. Making the connections. I don't think there's any emotion behind it.'

Gandalf continued to not move.

'I can only conclude little friend that some roads are blocked off for a reason. Ashley Heights is one of those roads. I think it's time I told the cartographer to erase that particular street from the A to Z of my feelings.'

After a moment Gandalf stood and trotted off Kieran's chest. Kieran got up and opened the curtains. The day outside was cloudy, drab and grey. It had rained in the night and the ground outside was almost completely obscured by golden brown, soggy leaves, as well as the occasional spent firework. The early November trees were looking more skeletal and pathetic with every passing day.

Gandalf started yowling to be let out of the living room, so Kieran opened the door, and the cat bolted in the direction of the kitchen.

Ashley was in there. She was wearing one of his shirts and frying bacon and eggs for sandwiches. The cafetiere was poised with ground coffee, ready for the water. The kettle was boiling, and there lay eight buttered white slices on the worktop. She was a vision of perfection. He could have framed her right then and he would have been eternally content.

'I hope you don't mind that I let Gandalf into the living room this morning. He was miaowing to go in. I guess he can't be away from you for very long eh?'

'No that's fine. I'm sure he just wanted to gently remind me that I haven't fed him yet.'

'And I stole one of your shirts.'

'Not a problem. You look better in it than I do.'

'That's a nice thing to say,' she smiled. 'And I borrowed your keys and nipped up to the shops to get some breakfast,' she said. 'Is that okay?'

'Of course it is. This is great. Just what I need actually. Is there anything I can do to help?' Kieran went over to the fridge and removed a half opened can of Whiskas.

'Nope, it's all under control. Listen, I was thinking,' Ashley said. 'If you aren't busy today we could take a trip into London after breakfast, to have a look at Crown Passage.'

'I'm not busy. That sounds like a good idea.'

'Excellent. Well sit down, this is nearly ready.'

~

They stepped off the Piccadilly Line train at Green Park. In the ticket hall a young homeless man was selling copies of The Big Issue, yelling, 'Please buy it. It's absolute shite really, I just need the munnneyyy.'

The tube had been flooded with tourists, and now the street - Piccadilly itself - was jammed with lost people looking at maps and queueing for sightseeing buses. The place seemed just as busy today as it did on a weekday.

The day had brightened somewhat and there was even a patch of blue directly overhead, but the mild wind of last night now had a chill in it. It had changed direction and was now coming from an Easterly direction. Londoners were beginning to get their first taste of winter.

Following the A to Z, Kieran and Ashley walked under the overhanging frontage of the Ritz Hotel, and turned right into Arlington Street, then left into Bennet Street. Soon they were on St James's Street walking down the hill towards St James's Palace.

As they walked Ashley talked about her holiday with Phillip in Fuerteventura. Kieran was interested in what she was saying, but he was only half listening. He was also thinking about David Everett and the boxes, and the absurdity of the notion that he could have been involved in all that. Kieran wondered if he really had the power to write letters, send cheques and make phone calls without being consciously aware of it. Perhaps a visit to the doctor was in order.

SPIRECLAW

He found himself paying more attention to Ashley when she mentioned that, while she and Phillip were on holiday the subject of marriage had come up.

'He didn't actually propose to me,' she was saying. 'I think he was just testing the water, gauging my reaction. We sort of discussed where we would live and how many kids we'd like to have.'

'And would you have married him? If he had asked?'

'Yes. Yes I probably would.'

They walked a little further, and soon they were standing at the northern end of Crown Passage, opposite the auctioneers and fine-art galleries on King Street. The passage itself was thin, with high buildings creating a closed-in, dark atmosphere. It ran for a couple of hundred yards joining King Street with Pall Mall. It appeared to have retained some of its historical charm, even though it was slowly giving way to modernity, as many London buildings eventually did.

They started down the passage, walking past a newspaper stand and a few small shops and restaurants, a newsagent, a barbershop and a Prêt a Manger.

They emerged out of Crown Passage on Pall Mall opposite St James's Palace and Marlborough House. Ashley was looking at some signs around the passage entrance, advertising some of the shops within.

'I wish I knew what we were looking for,' she said, shielding her eyes against a burst of sunlight that had quickly emerged from behind the clouds.

Kieran lit a cigarette and looked back along Crown Passage. 'This is silly.'

Ashley was biting her lip. 'I feel a bit silly too. Shall we just go?'

Kieran waved his hand dismissively. 'No. Not yet. We came a long way to see this place. I want to have another look.'

He began to walk up the passageway again, leaving Ashley behind. He walked past 'Hair To Go', the barbers. Opposite, there was a sandwich bar full of people buying lunch. An entrance nearby with a staircase led down to an underground wine bar called Davy's. At the King Street entrance to Crown Passage he turned again, looking more closely at shop fronts and signs, weaving in and out the passers by. Ashley caught up with him.

He looked at another sign that stood on the path outside a pub door; RED LION, CROWN PASSAGE, LONDON'S OLDEST INN, FINEST ENGLISH FAYRE, OVER 30 MALT WHISKEYS.

Ashley said. 'What do you...?'

'Hang on a sec.'

Kieran noticed he was shivering. He felt a strange sensation in his chest, almost like an excited feeling; an electrical feeling. He was beginning to feel as though the place was talking to him. But it wasn't Crown Passage that was communicating with him. It was all of London.

The notion came to his mind that the collective knowledge of everyone in the world was sufficient to answer his questions about Spireclaw and Edward Gosnell.

'Ashley we go through our lives, and we look for clues about its meaning. The answers are there. The answers often surround us but we don't know how to interpret them. And so we die more confused than we were when our lives began. London holds the answers to my questions. It's just a question of looking in all the right places.'

'Kieran are you okay?'

To Kieran, Crown Passage for a single moment ceased to exist. London was whispering.

Left pocket.

He felt as though he was tapping into the collective conscious of the city. He saw it for a moment. He glimpsed the stream of facts and truth that ran over the heads of all the people, like rivers of knowledge flowing in the sky, just out of reach. People in the passage brushed past him as they went about their business. Kieran was a rock in the middle of a babbling stream, the flow of people changing direction to go around him.

'Kieran?'

'Something about that sign,' he said, tapping his chin.

Ashley stared along the passage. 'What sign?'

Kieran pointed. 'That one. The Red Lion. I can feel it.'

Ashley read the sign. 'Well, what about it?'

'I don't know. I really don't know, I just...'

Kieran started patting his pockets, 'Where's that sheet of paper.'

He found it in his left pocket. The sheet of paper he had written the night before during the séance.

'Something about this paper.'

He unfolded it and looked at his writing.

ROW
KIERAN
NO
DEAD
NO
ROW
30MAL
ROWNPA
SSAG
CROWNPASSAGE

'Thirty malt whiskeys,' Kieran said, unable to suppress a smile. 'Thirty flipping malt whiskeys.'

Kieran handed the paper to Ashley and she read it. They looked at the Red Lion sign, and then they looked at each other.

'Do you reckon that's what it is?' said Ashley.

They were standing, static people amongst the transient crowd. They were connected to the stream. And now the direction of flow was clear.

'Definitely.' said Kieran.

'In that case I think we'd better go in,' said Ashley.

'Fancy a pint?'

~

The inside of the Red Lion was dark. It smelled of centuries of beer spilled on the ancient worn carpet, and had a red patterned cosiness that was common in old pubs. The place was empty but for an old man sitting at a table in the corner who looked like he'd been there since opening day, and the barman, who was reading a newspaper. The muted sound of footsteps outside merged with the ticking of a grandfather clock that perpetually knocked away at the lives of all who drank here.

Kieran and Ashley approached the bar and the barman looked up, smiling.

'What can I get you?' he said.

'I'd like a pint of Calders please,' said Kieran.

'I think I'll have a glass of dry white, thanks.'

The barman went about getting their drinks, and Kieran and Ashley looked at each other, sharing their bewilderment about what to do.

Ashley seemed to have more of a grasp of how to proceed than Kieran did. She came straight out with a question for the barman.

'Excuse me. I know this might sound odd but... does the name Edward Gosnell mean anything to you?'

The barman looked at Ashley, and didn't seem the least bit surprised to have been asked a question out of leftfield. Kieran guessed that as a barman he'd had to deal with stranger questions than this. He felt embarrassed nonetheless. He was glad Ashley was here. She possessed a level of courage that he only wished he had.

'Edward Gosnell,' said the barman, brushing back his thick brown hair. 'Edward Gosnell. No, I can't say it does.' He placed their drinks on the bar, 'Why do you ask? That'll be four-sixty.'

'I'll get this,' said Kieran, fishing for his wallet.

Ashley said, 'What about Spireclaw?'

The barman stopped momentarily and looked up into the sky of his imagination and memories. 'What's Spireclaw?' he said as he took the money from Kieran.

Then a raspy old voice, from the table in the corner, where the old man was sitting, said; 'Spireclaw! I'll bloody tell you what Spireclaw is.'

The three of them looked over at the old man, 'I haven't heard that word for sixty bloody years,' he said. 'But I can tell you what it is.'

SPIRECLAW

Kieran felt like an ice cube was running down his spine. He looked at Ashley. She was wide eyed, and she reached out and grabbed his hand tightly.

The barman leaned over the counter and whispered, 'That's my father.' Then he put out his hand, 'I'm Terry.'

~

Ashley asked the old man if she and Kieran could join him. He said yes and they took their drinks and pulled up two available chairs. He told them his name was Ernest Clarke. With an e.

He looked at Kieran through deep-set glassy eyes. The skin on his face and hands were almost reptilian with age, and his thin white hair was greasy and unkempt. He had a habit of running his fingers over his eyebrows, as if he was trying to flatten them.

'I was born during the First World War,' he said. '19 bloody 15. I joined Number Nineteen Squadron when I was twenty-three. Youngest bloody pilot they had I was. We were the first to fly the Dolphins. The Sopwith Dolphins. That's why our squadron badge had a dolphin on it. Still got the bloody thing somewhere. In a box in the attic. Now what was our motto? Ah yes. *Possunt Quia Posse Videntur*, They Can Because They Think They Can. That's right. Bit odd if you ask me. But when your best pals are getting shot down you didn't complain about the bloody motto.'

'You have the badge in your attic you say. Do you live here?' said Ashley.

'Nah. I live in High Barnet. Terry brings me down here every Saturday, to get me out of the house, y'know.'

'Was Spireclaw something to do with your time as a pilot?' asked Kieran.

Ernest Clarke's eyes looked skyward, seeking a distant part of his memory, same as the barman had. Kieran saw that the mannerism ran in the family.

'There were an awful lot of plane manouevres during 1940. An awful lot I tell you.' He flew his hand like an aeroplane above the table. 'We used to see single enemy planes buzzing the coast, usually late in the afternoon. Then, by the time dusk fell, there'd be twenty of 'em, dropping bombs and takin' out houses and roads. Even airfields.

'By then we weren't flying the dolphins. We had Spitfire Mark One's. Lovely birds they were. Lovely. But Spireclaw wasn't much of a big deal. No. It was one of them words we used when we wanted to refer to something. Squadron Leader Appleby thought it up, on account of the shape it would take.'

'Shape what would take?' said Ashley.

Ernest looked at Ashley accusingly, as though she hadn't been listening to a word he'd said. 'The manouevre of course!'

'What was the manouevre?'

Ernest took a gulp of his beer. 'It was July. A real scorcher. Not a bloody cloud in the sky. Appleby had received orders that we were to relocate five Spitfires out of Northolt. Take them over to Duxford for minor repairs. A hundred-and-thirty mile round-trip. Appleby called it Spireclaw. That was the name of the manoeuvre.'

'Why Spireclaw?'

'Like I said. Something about the shape. Five planes flying across the sky, like a claw. And the route we took, we flew over three churches. Used them as visual guides, like waypoints.'

'Where is Duxford?'

'Duxford's in Cambridgeshire. Got a museum up there now. Lovely it is to still see those beautiful birds fly. Bloody lovely.'

'Can you remember which churches were used? As waypoints?'

'Yes sir. Yes I can. The first one from Northolt was St John's Church in Buckhust Hill. Up in Borehamwood. Once you get airborne it's easy to see it there on the horizon. Then it was on to Essendon church near Hatfield. That one was a little harder to spot. And the last one, the most beautiful church was St Mary's in Saffron Walden. Once you saw that one you knew it was time to throw down those flaps.'

Kieran interrupted, 'What I don't understand is; why didn't you just use radios, or radar as navigational aids?'

SPIRECLAW

Ernest was beaming a wide smile. 'I was wondering when you was going to ask that question.' He rubbed his hands together mischievously and then parted them, holding them in the air above the table, seemingly to emphasise that he was about to make a very important point. 'We'd had orders from the top. The very, very top, that our communications signals were being monitored by the enemy. There were rumours flying about that either they had long-range radios picking up everything we said, or there were spies on the ground, hiding, and listening. The orders for radio silence were rescinded just a few days later, but at the time, everyone was scared, and no one wanted to take any bloody risks. We were losing enough planes as it was.'

'The men you flew with,' Ashley said. 'Were any of them called Edward Gosnell?'

Ernest shook his head. 'No love. Not at all. Never heard of him.'

~

Kieran and Ashley chatted to Ernest awhile longer. They heard more stories from the war. Terry the barman joked aloud that no one ever got away with hearing only one story, especially if they had asked for one in the first place.

A little later they came to the conclusion that there was nothing more that Ernest could tell them that would be of any use in their investigation. So they said their goodbyes and their thanks, and swapped phone numbers in case Ernest could remember anything else.

They walked out of the Red Lion, up Crown Passage and headed home. Ashley held Kieran's hand most of the way.

'I'm more confused now than I ever was,' said Kieran as they walked. 'Spireclaw was just a manoeuvre to get five planes from one base to another for some repairs during the war. I mean, how does that relate to all this. It's like someone's playing a damn joke on us. On me. I've reached that point again. That point where I'm beginning to wonder if I'm wasting my time with all this. Ashley, am I looking too hard for something that isn't there?'

'Kieran...'

'I could be looking in the haystack forever, only to find that the needle was never in it.'

'Kieran...'

'Yet all the time, I feel like I'm one step away from knowing something that will make all of this worthwhile.'

'Kieran! You have to continue looking. You need to find out why the word Spireclaw appeared in your cellar. You need to find out who Edward Gosnell is. You need to find out whether you really did ask David Everett to send those boxes to your work. And if you did, then why?"

Kieran stopped on the pavement and looked at her for a moment. The smell of traffic fumes reached his nostrils and he had fight back a sneeze. 'I've been thinking about that. I wanted to ask you. Do you have a video camera?'

'A video camera? No but they might have one at the studio.'

'Do you think they'd let you borrow it?'

'Sure, they're usually cool about that sort of thing.'

'And if they let you borrow it, would you let me borrow it?'

Ashley jumped in front of him and grinned. 'I think I know where you're going with this.'

~

'Directory Enquiries, how can I help you?'

'Yes. Good morning. I'm looking for the number for Duxford War Museum.'

Tapping keys. 'Is that Duxford in Cambridgeshire?'

'Yes.'

'I have the number. Would you like me to put you through?'

'Yes please.'

Ringing on the line.

A man's voice. 'Imperial War Museum Duxford. Chris speaking.'

'Yes, good morning. This may seem like a strange request but I'm wondering if you can help. Does the museum hold documents about the Aircraft repairs that were carried out there during 1940.'

'Well sir, every document that was ever generated by the base when it was in operation is stored in our archive. At the moment the archive itself is not open to the public. We don't have the facilities.'

'I see.'

'We are in the process of digitizing all of it, after which it will be available through our website.'

'How long will that be?'

'We don't anticipate going live with it until well into next year.'

'Oh, that's such a shame. It will be too late by then. Is there any way at all I can get access to any of the information? You see. It's my grandfather's ninetieth birthday next month and he flew Spitfires out of Northolt in 1940. He brought planes over to Duxford for repairs. I'm just trying to rustle up some memorabilia for him, as a surprise. Maybe get something framed.'

'Oh right. Listen, let me see if I can find anything for you. What's his name?'

'Ernest. Ernest Clarke. With an e.'

'Sometime in July 1940 he was ordered by Squadron Leader Appleby to relocate five planes over to Duxford. I'm trying to get access to the documents, to see if there are any references to the word Spireclaw on any of the papers.'

'Spireclaw?'

'It was the name of the manoeuvre. I don't know if it was an official name or not.'

'Okay. Ernest Clarke, Spireclaw, Appleby 1940. Do you happen to know which Squadron?

'Nineteen I think.'

'Okay. July 1940 you say."

'Yes.'

'Can you be more specific?'

'Not really. He's a bit hazy about it himself, being so old.'

'Okay, well listen Mr err...'

'Kieran. Kieran Whyteleafe.' He spelled out his surname, on account of the fact that nobody ever got it right first time. Kieran also gave his phone number.

'Let me get back to you in a couple of days. I don't mind having a look down there in my tea break.'

'I'm most grateful Chris.'

15

'Don't you think it's just crazy that we had a séance and it led us to Crown Passage, and then we found out what Spireclaw means? Don't you think that's just plain bonkers?'

It was the following Tuesday, and Ashley had arrived at Kieran's flat in a taxi with the video camera, housed in a battered metal case. Gandalf was pleased to see her, he kept milling around her legs, almost tripping her up a number of times.

'Yes,' said Kieran in reply. 'It is most definitely bonkers. But it's good. It means we're getting closer to a fundamental truth about the whole thing. It means we're making some damn progress.'

Kieran carried all the equipment into his bedroom. The case, a tripod and a bag of cables. Then he made Ashley a cup of tea while she unpacked it all and started to set it up. He didn't even bother trying to help; he didn't have the mind for that sort of thing.

When he brought in her mug she was just finishing. She screwed the tripod clip onto the base of the camera. Then she snapped the clip and camera into its housing on top of the tripod.

'There. I've set the timer to come on at Eleven pm. Hopefully you'll be asleep by then. It's a three hour tape, but if I set it to Long Play you'll get six hours out of it, which is most of the night.'

'Thank you Ashley. I really do appreciate this.'

'Not a problem. Don't forget to leave the light on or you won't see any of the footage when you watch it back. Now, do you want me to stay tonight?'

Kieran was shaking his head. 'I think it would be better if you left, y'know, for the experiment. I might be more relaxed.'

She regarded him for a moment, and he realised how that must have sounded.

'Why? Do I make you... not relaxed?'

'No, it's not that. No, that's not what I meant. Sorry. Forget I mentioned it.'

She nodded, and she was smiling. 'Don't worry. I think you're right anyway.'

~

Ashley left at about nine, and Kieran watched some television before going to bed. It took him a long time to get to sleep. He had to try very hard to forget that the camera would be watching him sleep. The idea made him feel quite self-conscious.

Eventually the balance tipped the other way as the weight of sleep made him less self-consciousness, and eventually he wasn't aware of anything.

~

Kieran's eyes flickered open. He was slightly startled to see the lights still on in his room. He wiped some sleep dust from the corner of his eyes.

A thin man in a long white coat was standing at the end of his bed. The man was looking at him. His hair was brown, poking out from beneath a small cap. He had sharp features, but nonetheless was quite attractive.

Kieran sat up abruptly, his nerves a pile of hot ashes. 'Who the hell are you?'

The man was touching the end of Kieran's bed lightly with his fingers. In the other hand he was holding out a ring, pinched between his thumb and index finger.

For a brief moment Kieran thought he'd seen the man before. He was momentarily convinced that he knew who the man was. But right now the figure didn't really seem there enough.

'What are you doing in my room?' whispered Kieran.

The man started to turn away, and faded into nothing as he did so.

Kieran watched the man disappear. His heart was thumping.

Had he just seen a ghost?

He took a couple of long, slow, deep breaths and looked around the room, then returned his gaze to the place where the man had been.

He rubbed his eyes. 'Jeeesus. What's wrong with me?'

He thought about the tape, still turning in the camera.

~

Kieran pressed the Eject button on the video camera and took out the little VHS-C tape. Then he placed it into the converter that Ashley had given him the night before. The converter allowed him to slot the tape into his own video recorder.

Kieran switched on the television, sat back on the sofa and pressed Play on the remote control.

And there he was, already sleeping, framed perfectly in the centre of the screen by Ashley's cinematographic prowess.

Kieran smiled. The sleeping TV version of him was snoring heavily. His mouth was open, dribbling pathetically onto the pillow. He thought he looked like a stupid old man.

Kieran fast-forwarded the tape. It was rather comical watching himself flipping over quickly in the bed like a sausage being cooked on all sides.

Kieran looked at the timer on the video recorder. He'd forwarded approximately an hour into the tape.

He looked back at the screen.

The bed was empty.

Kieran nearly jumped out of his skin. 'Eh?'

He pressed the Pause button, then Rewind. A few moments later the TV version of Kieran walked backwards into the frame and climbed backwards into bed.

Kieran pressed the Play button.

SPIRECLAW

The TV Kieran is asleep. He opens his eyes abruptly and stares at the ceiling. He lifts the duvet aside and swings his legs out of bed. His body has a rigidity that's normally missing from his posture. He stands up and walks out of frame.

He is gone for three minutes.

When he returns, he perches on the end of the bed. His posture is slightly pathetic; like that of a small child who has been told to go to his room.

Now he is pretending to hold something in his left hand. Something small and fiddly. With his right hand he is doing something to the imaginary thing in his left. Occasionally he shakes his right hand, as if it is cold and he is trying to warm it.

A minute or so later he stops abruptly. He looks up, in the direction of the wardrobe, but his eyes are blank. He doesn't seem to see anything in the room. He seems to see beyond its walls. He looks afraid.

A few moments later he climbs back into bed, pulls the covers over him and finds enough comfort to continue sleeping.

Kieran wound the tape forward to the end of the recording, thinking that the strange man in white might have been caught on tape.

At the point in the tape where Kieran sits up abruptly in his bed having just woken up and seen the strange figure, he is staring off camera at the end of the bed, at an unseen part of the room that was never meant to be captured by the lens.

Kieran pressed Stop on the tape. The TV flipped back to BBC1; some home improvement programme. The volume was too high and it jolted Kieran out of his trance. He looked down at his hands. They were shaking. They felt like alien appendages. New limbs, capable of activities he couldn't understand. He stood up and walked out to the kitchen, poured himself a stiff Jack Daniels, and knocked it back in one. Then he lit a cigarette.

The clock on the wall said 3:18am.

~

The following morning Kieran telephoned Mr Cray at the office and informed him that he wouldn't be able to make it into work today because he had a doctor's appointment. It was a little white lie as he had not made any such appointment but Mr Cray was okay with it and that was all that mattered.

Kieran hung up the phone and looked out of the window. The morning outside was heavily overcast and cold, and rainstorms waited menacingly on the horizon to wash the streets of London. Kieran stood in his dressing gown in the kitchen on the phone to the doctor's surgery. Gandalf milled around his legs, and his little warm cat body was comforting.

The lady at the surgery told him he could go down there straight away and wait to be seen.

He showered away his tiredness, got dressed into a pair of jeans and pulled on a white t-shirt. Then he ate a bowl of muesli as quickly as he could and bolted out the door. He was in the waiting room at the surgery by nine, surrounded by young mothers reading old copies of Hello and children playing with colourful toys on the heavily worn carpet.

He hated the synthetic medicinal smell. He felt ill just being there. He looked at the two receptionists. Do they smell of surgeries when they go home? The same way a person who works on a fish and chip shop always smells of day-old grease?

After twenty minutes of waiting, picking nervously at the skin around his fingernails, wondering what he was going to say, his name was called and he found himself walking down a thin corridor to a tiny doctors office.

Dr Thrower was very tall, and thin like the corridor to his office. He couldn't have been a day over thirty. He had the most infectious wide smile Kieran had ever seen on an NHS doctor. He had been Kieran's GP for as long as Kieran had been living in Northfields, which was about four years. Right now Kieran was glad he was speaking to a doctor who knew him, and although he had been lucky enough over those years not to have suffered from anything more severe than conjunctivitis two years ago and a minor ear infection last year, at least he and Dr Thrower were not complete strangers.

'Right. What seems to be the problem?'

SPIRECLAW

'I think I'm... performing activities in my sleep.'

'Do you mean sleepwalking?'

'And then some,' Kieran smiled.

'Do you have any examples?'

'Making phone calls to people I don't know. Writing letters. Last night I videotaped myself sitting at the end of my bed doing something with my hands.' He imitated the motion with his hands to show the doctor. 'I even thought I saw someone standing in my room.'

'Okay,' said Dr Thrower, nodding slowly.

'Frankly I'm pretty afraid that I might do something dangerous in my sleep.'

'Fine. Well, this isn't uncommon. There have been more cases of this sort of thing lately. Do you work long hours?'

'Yes, I work in a post room.'

'Stress and anxiety can be the main causes of sleep activity.'

Kieran nodded. 'I've had my fair share of that lately.'

'In what way?'

'My best friend. He committed suicide about three weeks ago.'

'I'm sorry to hear that. Was it after your friend died that you noticed that you were having trouble with your sleep?'

'No, I was doing it before. I called this guy, and sent him a cheque about two weeks before Phillip died.'

'You sent him a cheque?'

'It's a long story. I'm just wondering if there's any way I can control it.'

'Okay. Sleep activity is usually harmless. Like dreams it's just the subconscious mind trying to resolve little conundrums in your head. I'm going to prescribe you some short-acting tranquilizers to help prevent sleepwalking. You need to take one every night before you go to bed. Does your house have stairs?'

'No I live in a ground floor flat.'

Dr Thrower began to write out a prescription on his notepad. 'Good. Make sure you lock your front door at night. That will minimize the risk of you causing yourself an injury.' Dr Thrower smiled. 'And hide your chequebook.'

'Thank you. Are you sure these tranquilizers will help. I think I can be pretty resourceful when I'm asleep.'

Dr Thrower shook his head and continued to write. 'I think these will help a lot.'

16

On his way home from the underground station the following evening after work, Kieran broke into a run. He could hear the telephone ringing in his kitchen.

Stupid, he thought, and impossible too. He was, after all, about six houses away.

He carried on running anyway, and when he put the key in the lock on his front door, he realised that the phone actually *was* ringing in his kitchen.

He dashed through the door, dropped his bag and ran to pick it up.

'Hello?' he said, breathing hard.

'Hello. Please may I speak with Kieran Whyteleafe?'

'Speaking.'

'Hello, it's Chris from the Imperial War Museum in Duxford.'

'Oh hi, Chris. Hello. Thanks very much for getting back to me.'

'Not at all. I wanted to let you know, I've done a little digging into your grandfather's background here at the base.'

'Did you manage to find anything?'

'As a matter of fact I did. A total of nine planes were flown into Duxford for repairs in July 1940. Three of them came in on the fifteenth. The works order has the names of the pilots, as does the clearance sheet. Ernest Clarke is listed as one of the pilots, and the manoeuvre was instigated by Squadron Leader Mark Appleby based at Northolt.'

'Is there any mention of Spireclaw?'

'Well, not in any official capacity.'

'What do you mean?'

'Spireclaw was never an official name for the manoeuvre. None of the typed sheets refer to it. But someone has handwritten Spireclaw with a pen, in the corner of one of the sheets. I've checked the handwriting and it looks like Corporal Gittens wrote it. He was in charge at the time.'

'Would you be able to send me copies of those sheets. I would really love to frame them for my grandfather. I think he would love that. I will happily pay.'

'There's no need for that. I think the museum can afford an envelope and a stamp.'

'I'm very grateful. Here's my address...'

17

The sound of the telephone shocked Gandalf into a frenzy of tail-chasing and general cat lunacy, resulting in the little white monster colliding with the door of the kitchen, at which point he realised his stupidity and slinked off towards the living room.

'Gandalf you're an idiot!' said Kieran as he turned off the hob underneath the baked beans he was cooking and crossed the kitchen to answer the phone, flicking the tea cloth in his hand over his shoulder.

'Hello?'

'Kieran mate it's Tim.'

'Hello Tim, how are you?'

'Not too bad at all squire. Listen, are you up for Boy's Night Out this Friday? It's probably the last one before Christmas now. People will be buggering off to other parties and going on holiday and stuff so we want to get everyone together for one last piss-up.'

'Sure. Sound's messy, and good.'

'Nice. So don't forget to bring in a change of clothes so you don't look like an office tosser when we hit the bricks.'

'Okay. I'll remember.'

'Cool, see you tomorrow.'

There were six of them, and they went to the Buzz Bar in Panton Street. On a Friday night the bar was full of office lads like them looking for a shag, and girls trying to outdo each other in the provocative clothing stakes. Usually on "Boy's Night Out", practically all of the boys scored, but Kieran was never usually among the ones who succeeded in getting into a clinch with a member of the opposite sex. He just wasn't very good at it. He knew he only *thought* he had more style than his creators had actually blessed him with.

Once they all found a place to sit for the evening, a base from which the boys could attempt to pull girls, get rejected and then retreat back to before trying again elsewhere, Kieran and Darren went up to the bar to get drinks.

'What're you having?' shouted Kieran, keen to get the first round and then not have to worry for the rest of the evening.

'Me? I'll have a bottle of Spireclaw please.'

Kieran's nerves jumped. Ice shivers traversing his veins. 'A what?'

'I said I'll have a bottle of Stella please,' Darren shouted over the thumping rhythm of the music. 'You've gone a bit pale mate. Are you okay?'

'How can you tell in this light? No honestly I'm fine. It's just been a weird time lately.'

Darren nodded. 'I heard about your friend. That must have been pretty nasty. Losing a mate like that.'

'Kieran nodded. It's tough, but also pretty difficult to know how to act. Sometimes I feel like I'm lucky I didn't get into a situation like that.'

'You mean the fact that he...'

'The fact that he killed himself. Yes.'

Darren nodded. 'It is pretty messed up for sure. Imagine what his parents must be going through.'

'I dread to think. So that's one bottle of Stella for you. One for me. What did the others want?'

'A Newcastle Brown and three Becks.

Kieran paid for the drinks and the two of them carried the drinks back to the others at the table.

Other than Tim, Darren and Kieran, the other three lads were Tom, Jake and Dean, who all worked in the IT department at the same company. When the drinks arrived courtesy of Kieran, the three of them were engaged in a heated discussion about something called Active Directory DNS replication. It all sounded incredibly technical and Kieran's mind seemed to automatically blank itself to what was being said.

Darren said. 'You mentioned he left behind a girlfriend.'

Kieran nodded. 'They were living together. She came home one night and found him dead on the sofa. He'd drunk half a bottle of cleaning fluid.'

'Jeeeezus. Why would anyone do something like that?'

Kieran was shaking his head.

'I met the girlfriend at the funeral, and we went out after and got hammered. It was really odd.'

'Is she a sort?'

Kieran nodded, looking out across the crowded dance floor. 'We've sort of been out a few times.'

'No way!' said Tim. 'How come you never mentioned this at work?'

Kieran shrugged. 'Never seemed appropriate. Besides. I'm not really sure how I feel about it. It's a bit crazy. I feel like I've betrayed him, y'know. Like maybe she should be out-of-bounds.'

Tim threw his hands into the air. 'I don't think you should worry about it mate. If she's okay with it, and especially if she's a sort. Then everything's okay.'

Kieran and Darren stared at Tim. Kieran was unsure what to say.

Tim rocked his head from side to side, as though attempting to reason his way to safety. 'Okay, but look. He obviously didn't want to be with her. Otherwise he wouldn't have...'

Tim's eyes darted back and forth between Darren and Kieran. 'I'll get my coat shall I?'

November gave way to December, and where leaves once lay on the soggy morning ground, now it was the early winter frost, giving the days an icy, hollow, desolate opening when the clouds were gone and the lonely crescent moon hung in the pastel morning sky.

Christmas was approaching fast. Decorations were appearing in windows. Little pockets of flashing happiness telling the world that there was fun to be had, and soon.

After the day in Crown Passage, the conversations with Duxford Museum, and the night with the video camera, Kieran's dual investigation into Spireclaw and Edward Gosnell became less busy. This was due to Ashley taking a few weeks compassionate leave off work to go and see her aunt in America. She would be returning just after Christmas. She said she needed to get away from London to take stock. Her grief over Phillip came in waves for her, and she said she found there were times when she couldn't even muster the motivation to get out of bed. Kieran was surprised to discover this, because he had always thought she had been dealing with it so well.

She had clearly shown him her brave face.

Kieran found that his own grief over Phillip was numb and unquantifiable, and he felt fairly sure that the numbness was quite common amongst people who grieved. He hated to admit it but he found it difficult to miss his friend. They had not seen very much of each other over the past few years, what with Phillip travelling so much and the two of them having quite distinct and separate lives.

Christmas Day arrived. The world outside - as ever at Christmas - possessed a muted stillness devoid of cars and life.

In the morning, Kieran telephoned Diane Hynes to say hello and let them know that he was thinking of them. Their first Christmas without Phillip was undoubtedly going to be hard for them. They chatted for about five minutes and Diane thanked him for the card he had sent.

Later on, Kieran cooked a turkey for him and Gandalf, although he only cooked enough potatoes, parsnips, sprouts and carrots for himself. Gandalf - for some reason - was never interested in the vegetables unless it was mange-tout.

Gifts for Kieran came in a box from his mother in Cape Town. A Springbok rugby shirt which he couldn't imagine himself ever wearing, three cans of Milo which he couldn't imagine himself ever drinking, and a Panic Mechanic video which he couldn't imagine himself ever watching. His mother had also included a long newsy letter about the latest golf-club gossip. Such-and-such this and so-and-so that. All people that Kieran had never met. People whose lives were just words on a page to him.

Gandalf and Kieran sat down to eat just before the Christmas film started on the television. Kieran had barely picked up his knife and fork when the phone began to ring.

He dropped his cutlery down noisily on the plate and looked resignedly at Gandalf, who was happily dragging a piece of turkey across the carpet.

'Bugger', he said, and put his plate aside.

It was Ashley. 'Merry Christmas!' she bellowed into his ear from four thousand miles away.

'Ashley! Merry Christmas. I wasn't expecting to hear from you.'

'Well. If I must be honest I wasn't planning on calling.'

'Oh, thanks!'

'But I have some very interesting news.'

'What kind of news?'

'Are you having a good Christmas? How's Gandalf?'

'He's good. Right now he's tucking into his Christmas lunch. So what's the news?'

'And you're okay? Did you hear from your Mum?'

'Yes I did. Loads of lovely presents and a letter to put War and Peace to shame. Ashley, what's the news?'

'Oh Kieran you are an impatient so-and-so! I was enjoying keeping you in suspense.'

Kieran waited.

Ashley remained quiet.

The silence got longer. He could imagine her grinning at the other end of the line.

They both burst into laughter.

'Well?' said Kieran, still laughing.

'Okay okay. Make sure you're sitting down,' she said, 'Because. Well, you're not going to believe this, but I think I've found out who Edward Gosnell is.'

Kieran dropped the handset. It clattered on the table and skidded onto the floor.

'Shit!'

When he rescued it and put it to his ear, he could hear Ashley laughing again at the other end of the phone.

'Did you just drop it?' she said.

'Yeah. Did you say you've found Edward Gosnell?'

'Not exactly found, no. But I think I know who he is.'

'He's in the States?'

'In the States,' she said.

'What are the chances of that? I mean, how do you know it's the same guy.'

'Well, in truth, I don't. But you said yourself there aren't any Edward Gosnells listed in the UK.'

'Well, there might be ex-directory ones.'

'Fair enough. But wait till you hear about this one. I've got a newspaper article here, from nearly thirty years back. Can I read it to you?'

Kieran thought about his lunch, getting cold in front of the Christmas film. Then he visualised it being reheated in the microwave. 'It's your phone bill, Ashley.'

'Actually it's my aunt's, but she doesn't mind. Okay, now. This article's in a newspaper dated Tuesday 15th May 1973. I got it from the library archives. Edward Gosnell's a bit of a local hero round here. Bit of a martyr. He's quite well known.'

'So what's the story?'

'Okay, here's what it says. Hang on. "Protests over the execution of Edward Gosnell three days ago have shown no signs of abating. The gathering of two hundred people outside the Lubbock Texas Town Hall are adamant that Gosnell's conviction is both unjust and barbaric. Edward Gosnell 29, was executed in the electric chair on Saturday May 12th for

SPIRECLAW

murdering three young men; Jonathan Parry, Michael Rosen and Randy Brecker outside the Holy Road truck-stop twenty miles northeast of Lubbock. Gosnell had always maintained that he had caught the three men intimidating his wife Mandy Gosnell and preparing to perform unlawful sexual intercourse with her in the parking lot outside the diner. Gosnell was found guilty of shooting the three men. The husband and wife maintain that the shooting was to prevent the rape.

Each of the three men had been accused and acquitted...'"

~

...of previous rape charges. Judge Wendell Holmes refuted Gosnell's claims, stating that the previous cases against the men resulted in innocent verdicts, and therefore he did not condone Gosnell's "own sense of misguided justice. The protests continue."

Kieran finished reading the photocopy of the newspaper article and dropped it on the table. He looked up at Ashley. They were sitting at a little table near the back in Jackson's Bar on a bitterly cold, cloudless evening. It was the eve of New Years Eve.

Kieran tapped the page. 'This guy was executed on my birthday.'

Ashley nodded. 'That was what made me take notice.'

'But don't you think it would be a bit of a huge coincidence that you happen to go out to the States and accidentally stumble across the very Edward Gosnell we're looking for?'

'Yes, true,' she said slowly. 'But hasn't this whole thing been about coincidences. Spireclaw popping up like that, twice in your life. You deciding to ring Phillip out of the blue on the day he... on the day he...'

Kieran flattened both of his hands on the piece of paper and leaned forward. 'But Ashley, what possible significance can this murdering hick from Texas have to do with all of this.'

Ashley was rubbing her forehead. 'I don't know Kieran, but don't you feel it's all connected in some convoluted way?'

Kieran could feel tension in his shoulders. He let them slump and sighed.

'That day in Crown Passage. I could feel something. A presence. A force. Some sort of connection. Or even a sense of belonging. Maybe it was the same force that was present at the séance the night before. That same force that guided us towards Crown Passage in the first place. The more the pieces begin to fit into place the more I can feel this thing, this force, this presence. It's trying to tell me something. And I think that deep down in my body, somewhere in the darkest, most inaccessible parts of my soul, lies the answer to this. That's the strange thing about it. I feel like I already know the answer, or part of me does. Some secret part of me. I just don't know how to get it all out into the open.'

Ashley took a sip of her vodka cranberry and glanced self-consciously around the bar, and Kieran wondered if his empassioned speech about the mystery of it all had been too loud. Then she said. 'The thing that puzzles me now is, if this Edward Gosnell guy really is the one we've been looking for all along, and even if he isn't, why on Earth would you ask David Everett to write his name on the side of all those boxes?'

'I don't know.'

'I mean, what special hold has Edward Gosnell got over you?'

Kieran shrugged. 'Maybe he's a... a distant relation.'

'I don't know,' said Ashley. 'We might not have the right man.'

'I'm beginning to feel that we have.' said Kieran.

'You've changed your tune.'

'So have you.' Kieran shook his head. 'Regardless. If this is the right Edward Gosnell, and I must say I wasn't expecting the bloke to be dead, then we've pretty much exhausted all our options, because I have no idea where to go from here.'

Ashley nodded. 'We should continue looking for other Edward Gosnells.'

'And then we're back where we started,' said Kieran. 'Spireclaw's a dead-end right? Some lame RAF maneouvre during the Battle of Britain.'

'Not even that, just a jaunt for repairs.'

'And Edward Gosnell's a guy from Texas who got the chair nearly thirty years ago for blowing away three guys he alleged were going to rape his wife. If it's the right guy.'

'Yep.'

'And somehow they keep turning up in my life like a couple of bad pennies.'

Ashley was nodding. 'Looks like we're still missing something important, don't you think?'

'Part of me still thinks this is a puzzle with no solution. Like the jigsaw box came with half the pieces missing, rendering it impossible to finish.'

'Well, it's definitely something to do with the war. The Second World War. You have a pile of newspapers from the war, and the word Spireclaw is a wartime term.'

'Yes but the times don't match. The Duxford repairs took place during The Battle of Britain, in July 1940. The newspaper was 1943. No correlation whatsoever.'

Ashley gazed out of the window at the empty street, thinking. 'Unless the correlation is implied.'

'Implied?'

'Yeah. You said you couldn't see any instances of the word Spireclaw in the newspaper.'

'Well, I scoured the whole thing.'

'Okay so maybe there's something in-between. Something that connects Spireclaw to something in the paper.'

Kieran was scratching his head. 'I don't see how we'd ever pin something like that down.'

Ashley placed her fists against her temples, as if such an act aided thought. 'One thing we can be sure of though. If the Edward Gosnell I found in Texas is the one we've been looking for, then the newspaper isn't going to have any articles about him.'

'True. And I did check it for his name already and found nothing.'

'After all, the guy wasn't even born then, right?'

'No. He would have been... well, if he was twenty-nine when he was executed on May 12th 1973, then on October 15th 1943 he wouldn't have been born yet.'

'Well, hang on. He could have been. His thirtieth birthday would have been sometime in the year following his execution.'

Kieran was shaking his head. 'Trying to tie these dates together is completely pointless I'm sure. Yet again we're looking for things that just aren't there.'

Ashley placed her elbows on the table and her head in her hands, her wide open eyes blinking sweetly. 'I like it though.'

'Why?'

'Because it helps me take my mind off Phillip.'

They regarded each other in silence for a moment. The collective noise of all the people in the bar filled Kieran's head, and for a moment he imagined that he was listening to the babbling voices of dead people. Each one trying to say the things they never had the time or courage to say when they were alive.

'By the way,' Kieran said, reaching into his pocket. 'I received the documents from the Imperial War Museum in Duxford.' He pulled out the two sheets of paper that Chris had sent him. He handed them to her and she unfolded them.

'It verifies the names of the churches they flew over. But no mention of Spireclaw.'

'It's on the other sheet. Handwritten at the bottom.'

Ashley looked at the other sheet. 'Oh right.'

'I think I might get them framed actually, and give them to Ernest. I think he might like that.'

'That'll be nice,' Ashley nodded. 'Oh I almost forgot.'

'What?'

'We're having a party for New Year tomorrow at my parents place,' she said. 'Would you like to come? That is, if you don't have any other plans.'

Kieran snapped out of his semi-trance and shook his head, 'I don't have any other plans. I'd love to come.'

~

Kieran stood on the doorstep under the welcoming beam of the porch light. He pressed the doorbell with a gloved hand and watched through the frosted glass at some bodies moving at the other end of the hall. The movement merged into the

SPIRECLAW

shape of Ashley, which grew in definition as she hurried to the door. When she opened the door the music from inside the house grew in definition too. Now that he could hear the treble in the sound he could tell that the song was "Labour of Love" by Hue and Cry.

Ashley smiled, and to Kieran she seemed immaculate just then. She had a new hairstyle and must have just got it done today. It was a layered bob; a style Kieran loved on women, and now she was confirming the reason why he loved it. She was wearing the black suit-trousers she wore at the funeral, high heels, and a small burgundy crop-top with tiny thin shoulder straps. A brief downward glance at her invitingly exposed navel revealed a pierced belly button. A heart-shaped necklace lay invitingly across her sternum. He wanted nothing more right then than to kiss her.

'It's you!' she grabbed his hand, eyed him coquettishly and led him quickly into the house, making him almost trip on the doorstep. He removed his coat and hung it on one of the hooks by the door.

They went into the kitchen. It was one of those large sprawling kitchen and dining areas; full of people Kieran didn't know. He was surprised at the turnout given that there was still another four hours to go until midnight. Numerous plates of common-or-garden party food were laid out all over the sideboards. Ashley hurriedly loaded a paper plate with sausage rolls, crisps, peanuts and small strips of breaded chicken and planted it in Kieran's hand. In his other hand she placed a bottle of Becks.

'Thanks Ashley.'

She led him through to the living room, where her father and about seven other people were sat on the floor, crowded round a low roulette table.

'Dad got it for Christmas,' she said.

'Hello Kieran,' said Brian. 'Nice to see you under less sombre circumstances.' He stood up and shook Kieran's hand.

'Likewise Brian,' said Kieran. 'Good to see you, thanks for letting me come tonight.'

'Not at all. Perhaps you can help us with this damn roulette table.' He waved a piece of A4 in front of them. 'It's plain flippin' bonkers. The instructions have been translated from Japanese to English by someone who clearly has no comprehension of the nuances of either language. And the table itself has all French writing on it. And here we are left trying to figure out the rules because none of us have ever played it before.'

Ashley said, 'I was thinking Dad. Maybe we can find some more appropriate instructions on the Internet.'

Brian turned to the others gathered round the table. 'Now why the hell didn't I think of that? It must be some sort of generational quirk.'

Ashley giggled and grabbed Kieran's hand again, giving him the distinct impression that she was playing some sort of game with him. She whisked him through the living room door and along the corridor towards the stairs.

They went up to the first floor landing, past numerous closed doors, one of which - Kieran imagined - would be Ashley's bedroom. His mind performed a somersault at the thought. At his age, the mere idea of witnessing the secrets of a woman's bedroom was wholly tantalizing. Mysterious in the way that Samantha's phone number used to be when he sometimes stared at it in the phone directory, many months before he ever had the chance to kiss her. But thoughts of Ashley's bedroom would have to wait, because she had already towed him onto the next staircase. She was whisking him up into the loft conversion.

'What exactly does your father do?' said Kieran as he looked around the huge attic office he now found himself standing in.

The place was a mess of paper, scattered over the two large desks, though a lot of it had been stacked too high and too near the edges on the desk furthest from the entrance that lots of sheets had slipped off onto the chair or the floor.

'He's a solicitor.' said Ashley as she made her way over to the desk nearest the door - which had a computer on it - and sat down.

Kieran followed her, but as there was no other chair he remained standing, albeit with his head bent forward on

SPIRECLAW

account of the sloping attic roof. It was instantly uncomfortable so he bent his knees and crouched beside her.

Ashley moved the mouse on the desk and the monitor clicked on. Then she opened the Internet Explorer program. The Google search page appeared.

Kieran found himself watching her face more than the screen. He could smell her now. He was getting lost in her look and her perfume. These thoughts were swimming to the surface of his mind because it had been such a long time since he'd shared a bed with a woman. And never one as beautiful as Ashley. Phillip had been such a lucky man. Being in Ashley's house heightened every emotion that Kieran felt about the situation. Jealousy over Phillips ability to even catch a girl like this. Sadness because of the whole damn shitty circumstances that brought Ashley and he together. Longing because all he wanted to do was kiss her. But kissing her was the one thing he could not do. Or was it?

He watched her type the words 'Roulette rules' and click Go. Seconds later a screen of results appeared.

'This'll do.' said Ashley as she clicked into the first result, and sent it to the printer.

'Ashley, did you ever think of typing Spireclaw into a search engine?'

She looked down at him and shook her head, letting her hair fall in front of her face. 'It never occurred to me. Good idea.'

She tucked her hair behind her ears and typed "Spireclaw" on the keyboard.

The computer replied: "No search results match your criteria. Did you mean Spire Claw?"

'What about Edward Gosnell?' said Kieran.

She typed "Edward Gosnell".

The search results came up with a number of genealogy pages that had both the words "Edward" and "Gosnell", but only as the first or last half of a different name. Edward Finch and John Gosnell for example.

Ashley uttered a noise that was half titter and half tut. 'Nothing.' she said. 'Why am I not surprised?'

She turned her head back to him, and she saw now that he was staring at her. She was slightly taken aback, showing in her look that she had been expecting him to be looking at the screen, not at her.

After a moment she said: 'Kieran, we shouldn't.'

Kieran was tempted to drop his head, but instead chose to hold it instead. 'I just think... I want you to know that I...'

Her mouth moved to his. They were kissing before he even had a chance to realise. It was a short but intense encounter, acted out with relish and a little desperation from both sides.

She moved away slightly, but kept her face very close to his.

Kieran said 'Are we mad?'

Ashley shook her head, 'Not nearly mad enough.'

After a moment she stood up, picked up the pages off the printer and took his hand once again. She led him towards the stairs. 'Come on. They'll be wondering where on Earth we got to.'

~

They were standing in the living room when the clock struck twelve, ushering in a new year of choices and possibilities, Kieran wanted so desperately to kiss Ashley again, to let their embrace traverse the boundary between one year and another. It could have served as a marker. A shared moment of grief, which slowly became an expression of feeling and mutual passion. But there was another boundary they were both aware of, and Kieran could tell from the urgency of her look that she wasn't ready for her family to see that she and Kieran might have become more than just grieving friends.

He hoped it was something they might one day become aware of, and perhaps eventually become accustomed to.

~

A light snow was spiraling out of the orange sky when Kieran walked home later that night. In his mind he was full of the joys the New Year might bring. He was excited about the kiss.

Turning the corner out of Ashley's road he wondered whether their kiss had possessed any depth and dimension for her. It certainly did for him, and he thought it probably did for her, but as he replayed her actions and reactions in his mind, he could feel the doubt creeping in.

By the time he reached home - cold and tired - half an hour later he'd convinced himself through over-thinking that she had only kissed him because it seemed like a friendly thing to do at New Year, and that he'd been foolish, selfish and thoughtless to think differently.

Once inside, he walked into the kitchen and knocked back two pints of water to stave off the effects of the evening's alcohol. Then he fell into bed - forgetting to take a sleeping tablet - he was fully clothed, and unknowingly, for the first time in a long time, he slept a full ten hours and remained exactly where he was for the whole night.

18

Ah la la-la.
Summer rain is pouring down again,
And it's getting wetter.
As a matter of fact it couldn't be better.
For baby and me, sitting on my knee.

Kieran is sitting in the back seat of his Dad's red Ford Cortina and the two of them are singing loudly to a Chris de Burgh tape. All the windows are down and Kieran has his head near the window. The soft, quick hand of the wind is ruffling his hair and he loves the warm feeling of it on his face.

Kieran is six and they are driving to the seaside. Mum isn't around because this is Dad's weekend.

He reaches his hand into a small paper bag and pulls out two cola-cubes that are stuck together. He pulls them apart, replaces one and examines the other. The one he is about to eat has paper stuck to it. Kieran peels it off, flicks it out of the window and pops the sweet into his mouth.

Kieran can feel the excitement in the bottom of his tummy. He's imagining the bucket and spade in the plastic bag in the boot. He's remembering the flip-flops he put in with them; the flip-flops that still had sand on them from the last time he came to the seaside. He's remembering the games of chess he had on the verandah with grandpa that time. He's remembering the visit to the lifeboat station at the end of the road his grandparents live on, an ice-lolly melting quickly in his hand, sticky and running down his arm, all the way to his elbow.

The car is going slower now and Dad is making more turns. Kieran is beginning to recognise some of the bungalows on the road into the village. The pink one with ivy on the walls. The bright white one with the fast car parked in the driveway.

The signpost to the beach! Now that Kieran has seen it he leans forward and pokes his head between the seats, pressing his cheek against Dad's arm.

'Nearly there!' says Dad.

After a couple more turns, driving slower each time, they pull up outside the bungalow.

Dad's Mum and Dad are already at the door, they walk down the front path. Granny has her arms folded across her chest, hugging herself. Kieran thinks for a moment that she looks sad, even though she is smiling.

Grandpa is grinning like he always does. He is called Arthur. Arthur has the wrinkliest hands Kieran has ever seen, but Kieran likes him because he always has biscuits.

Arthur bends down to the open window of the car and puts his hands on his knees. 'Hello Kieran!'

Kieran smiles, 'Hello grandpa.'

Dad gets out of the car and walks over to the old couple. He hugs them both. Granny says 'Hello Graham. How was the drive down?'

'Seems like the world and his wife were on the A3 this morning,' he replied. 'But once we got past Guildford it was fine.'

SPIRECLAW

A fly buzzed lazily and aimlessly into the still heat of the car and out through another window.

'Would you like some orange squash?' Arthur said to Kieran.

'Yes please.'

'Well come on then! Out you get!'

~

Kieran is sitting cross-legged on the carpet in the lounge in a warm rhombus of sunlight. On the floor beside him sits a big glass of orange squash and a bag of Iced Gems. He is building a castle out of Lego, but the pieces he's been given are inadequate for the task. Granny and Grandpa obviously don't play with Lego. They got the dusty box of pieces down from the attic.

Later, after the grown-ups have talked, he will be allowed to go and play on the beach.

'Any trouble getting him for the weekend?' said Granny.

'My weekends with him are always pre-arranged. No problems there. But every time I go to collect him she's always asking for bloody money. I get so distraught before I go round there now, because there usually always is an argument. I had to go and see a bloody doctor about it.'

~

Grandpa takes Kieran down to the water, and sits on the bench on the sea wall reading the paper while Kieran paddles around at the water's edge. The tide is low and the sea is calm, and through the cold clear water, where sand oozes slowly over his wet feet, he sees a little crab burrowing out of sight. He reaches down to get a handful of sand, hoping to pick up the little creature, but his hands come up empty.

In the clear bright day the sound of a lawnmower carries on the breeze. Out to sea a speedboat bounces rapidly across the shimmering horizon, the sound of its hull impacting with the water delayed in reaching Kieran's ears. Further along the beach near to the massive wooden ramp of the lifeboat station, he sees some other children playing in a small inflatable dinghy. They are laughing loudly with excitement. Their mother and father are sitting on a blanket beside a windbreak further up the pebbly beach. Kieran wonders what it would be like to have a brother or a sister.

After an hour or so Grandpa calls Kieran up from the water's edge and they head back to the bungalow. The day is growing tired and lazy now. The shadows on the ground are getting longer and a low-flying plane has been buzzing over the water. As they walk along the road Kieran pretends he is a Spitfire, banking left and right, and gunning the ground. He makes the accompanying noises with the back of his throat.

When they go inside, Granny and Dad are talking. She is holding an audio cassette and she gives it to him.

'You can have this copy, it's lovely,' she said. 'You can play it to Kieran when he's much older.'

Dad nods, smiles and looks at Kieran. 'I'm sure he'll love that. I could play it to his future girlfriends. Thanks very much Mum, that's very kind. I'll just go and put it in the car so I don't forget it when we leave.'

~

The car journey home from the seaside seems much longer. But it's okay because they're listening to tapes.

Dad even plays him the tape that Granny gave him. It was recorded when Kieran was a baby. Kieran thinks it is funny to hear himself making baby noises.

When they arrive home, Kieran asks Daddy if he can take the Chris de Burgh tape out of the car to play inside.

Dad says yes and gets out of the car. Kieran climbs between the two front seats and ejects the tape. He also takes the other tape, now back in its box, lying on the floor in foot well of the front passenger seat. He doesn't really know why he's taking it. It's just one of those things that little boys do.

19

The following morning - January the first - Kieran woke up a little before midday. He felt surprisingly okay given that he'd had a fair amount to drink at the party.

He made himself some coffee and toast, fed Gandalf and sat in the living room watching television. Some sickly sweet children's Christmas family movie was showing, and he only half paid attention to it.

The first indication he had that his flat was being broken into was when Gandalf - who had jumped up onto his lap - lifted his head quickly and spun his ears through one-eighty degrees.

Then Kieran heard something being knocked over in the bathroom; probably one of the bottles on the windowsill. In an instant of defensive instinct, Kieran could feel white fear ripping through his veins.

Someone was climbing in through the bathroom window.

'Shit!'

Gandalf jumped down to the floor, ears still inverted, and slinked towards the living room door.

Kieran picked up the remote control to mute the volume on the television, but then thought better of it and put it down without touching any of the buttons. Better not to alert the intruder that he knew something was up. He cast his eyes around the room for something he could use as a weapon, if it came to such an eventuality. The best thing he could find was an empty bottle of Becks on the coffee table. He picked it up and held it by the neck, brandishing it.

The noise in the bathroom continued, the clatter echoing down the hall. More plastic bottles and cosmetic accoutrements were falling off the windowsill into the bath. Whoever was climbing in through the window couldn't have been any noisier if they tried.

As Kieran stepped out into the corridor he felt acid in his stomach rising to his throat and he grimaced as he swallowed it back.

Now he could see the door to the bathroom. It was ajar, and quick shadows were passing over the little patch of blue wallpaper that he could see inside the room.

He edged a little closer, raising the bottle slightly in case he might need to use it sooner than he thought. Gandalf was nowhere to be seen.

More things being knocked over. Kieran glanced at the kitchen. It's door was adjacent to the bathroom so from where he was he could see the phone hanging on the wall, next to a corkboard littered with pizza take-away flyers and mini-cab cards.

He considered heading for the kitchen instead. Perhaps he could quietly call the police.

No. Even if they came as fast as they could, he wouldn't be able to hide that long. He would have to confront the burglar no matter what. The situation was too immediate.

More clattering. Kieran was now right outside the bathroom door, heart hammering in his chest. Did he have the courage to push open the door? He wavered slightly, wondering if he should call out to whoever was inside.

The clattering of bottles stopped. Perhaps they had all been knocked into the bath by now. But there was a new sound.

Flapping clothes. No. Flapping wings. Thud. Thud.

Kieran pushed the door open wide to reveal the mess in the bathroom.

A pigeon flew at him. He ducked and it flapped straight over his head. The Becks bottle fell out of his hand.

'Bloody hell.'

He turned to see the pigeon flying down the corridor, bash heavily into the front door and spin back towards him. He dodged out of the way as it flew straight back into the bathroom.

Kieran bolted to the front door and opened it wide. The pigeon clattered about in the bathroom again before zooming back down the hall and straight out the front door. He followed it out and watched it soar upwards into the sky.

For a few moments Kieran stood on the porch holding his breath. Still in a state of shock, watching the bird disappear over the top of the house across the street.

Then, after a minute or so of letting his breathing and heart rate return to normal, he went back into the house and closed the front door.

All along the corridor the floorboards were messy with smatterings of pigeon droppings, but the bathroom was worse. As he had guessed from the noise, the bath was full of things that had fallen off the windowsill. Shaving foam, shampoo, his razor, his deodorant and assorted bottles of aftershave all pooled in a heap near the plughole, covered in pigeon crap, which had smeared all the way up the bath, up the wall and onto the carpet too.

'What a bloody mess Gandalf,' he said and went to make a cup of tea, into which he added two extra sugars, and sipped while he leaned against the jamb of the bathroom door, surveying the damage.

That was when he noticed that the bathroom window was closed. It had been closed all along. He turned and looked along the corridor.

'Well, how the hell did he get in?' he whispered to himself.

He walked into the kitchen. All the windows were closed. The bedroom windows were also closed. The only open window in the entire flat was the one in the living room, but he had been sitting in there, and he certainly would have noticed a pigeon flapping past on its way to the bathroom. And besides, the bathroom door wasn't open enough to allow the creature to get in.

Back in the kitchen he filled a bucket with hot water, washing up liquid and bathroom cleaner, donned a pair of rubber gloves and went into the bathroom to attack the stains.

He ran the taps in the bath and started to clean the pigeon shit off the bottles, taking each clean item and placing it back on the windowsill. He reached over to the lever to route the water up to the showerhead that hung on a hook above the bath.

But he didn't pull the lever because he saw something in the droppings that stopped him dead, and made him drop everything, dash to the kitchen, pick up the phone and call Ashley.

~

Ashley and Kieran stood in the bathroom looking at the mess of pigeon crap smeared across the white expanse of the bath.

Ashley looked exquisite and delicious, with ruffled hair, a thin black t-shirt and grey-green cargo pants.

'Can you see it?' he said, keen for some assurance that he wasn't going mad.

She tilted her head to one side. 'Well, if you squint a little perhaps.'

'Oh come on it's easier than that. Look,' he pointed. 'There's the S, and it runs all the way across to the W over there.'

Ashley was nodding. 'I know I can sort of see it. But it's a little like a Rorschach test isn't it? Open to interpretation.'

'No, it's much more obvious than that.'

Ashley let out a sigh. 'Well I don't really know what you want me to say, Kieran. All I can think of is how smelly it is in here. Come on, let's clear it up.'

Ashley worked on the bathroom while Kieran scrubbed away at the floorboards in the corridor. Every now and then while he was working away on his hands and knees, he would glance along the corridor and see her on her knees beside the bath. And for a moment everything seemed perfect. There was something so ordinary and domesticated about what they were doing that Kieran felt a strong rising feeling of groundedness and homeliness.

He had a glimpse of what life might be like if they were married. And for some crazy reason, tears welled up in his eyes.

Maybe it was because his feelings for her were growing stronger with each passing day, and every time he saw her he found another reason to want to be with her. Maybe it was because domestic bliss, even in the guise of the mundane things like cleaning up pigeon shit, was a thing that he had never seen his parents indulging in.

He fought back the emotion. He didn't want Ashley to see him with tears in his eyes; not when he couldn't explain their reason for being.

Before long he finished scrubbing the floorboards and went and stood in the bathroom doorway while Ashley finished off what she was doing. 'Thanks for helping and everything.'

'Oh that's okay.' She stood up and flicked her hair away from her face. Her cheeks were flush. She started to wash her hands in the sink.

Kieran said, 'Would you like to go for a walk. Maybe in Walpole Park. We could get some lunch after perhaps.'

~

The park was empty. The cold bare trees, the muddy dewey grass and sludgy soggy leaf-soaked paths were laid out by nature just for Ashley and Kieran. There was a thick cloud cover in the sky, which robbed the day of its colour, but reciprocated by taking some of the chill away too.

Kieran and Ashley entered the park from the Mattock Lane entrance and walked around the perimeter path. Ashley had linked her arm through his and it made him feel confident and safe.

Kieran looked across the park at the trees surrounded by ground mist and said. 'In the cold light of day, what do you think about last night? About what happened between us.'

'Do you want to know if I thought it was a mistake?'

'Well, yes, I do.'

Ashley was shaking her head. 'It wasn't a mistake. I'm glad we kissed. I think we both needed it.'

'But, Phillip would...'

'Phillip would be glad if I ended up with you.' Ashley moved her hand and slid it into the big pocket in Kieran's thick coat. She found his hand and netted her fingers between his.

He was looking at her. 'Do you really think so?'

She half shrugged. 'I don't know. I'd sort of hoped that he wanted me for himself. I guess I was wrong about that.'

Kieran wasn't sure what to say after that. He supposed he wanted to comfort her by saying that she surely wasn't any part of the reason Phillip took his own life. He wanted to tell her that she was too wonderful for that to be true. But he didn't want to try and placate her with flattery that would just seem - well, flat, under the circumstances, because the bottom line was this: Phillip took his life even though he knew Ashley was there for him. Ashley, therefore, was not enough of a reason for him to stay alive.

She seemed to sense his internal struggle and said, 'Don't worry. I'm not going to go all complex on you. I purged a lot of that stuff when I was in the States. I must have driven my poor aunt mad while I was there. Y'know, letting it all out and everything. I'm so glad I went though. I didn't realise how much I needed it until I actually got there.'

'I'm pretty amazed at how well you've dealt with it.'

'Well I've hidden the worst of it from you.'

'I thought that might be the case. I wish you wouldn't though.'

She gripped his hand a little tighter. 'It's automatic. I don't intend to be a certain way. That's just the way it happens. Don't you find sometimes that you experience emotions and moods that you don't understand? You end up following them, seeing where they take you.'

Kieran's mind returned to the bittersweet feelings he'd felt in the hallway back at the house, where he'd suddenly felt tears in his eyes just because he saw her scrubbing away at the bath. 'Yes,' he said. 'I know exactly what you mean.'

She stopped and he stopped too. She looked up at him, her eyes were filled with tears but she was smiling. It was a real, genuine, warm smile and she sniffed, pulled a tissue from her other pocket and wiped her nose. 'Still, we've all got to get on with it haven't we.'

Kieran nodded, he could feel his throat clenching up the way it often did before his eyes started to well up.

She said. 'Do you regret kissing me?'

'Ashley, I don't think anyone could ever regret kissing you.'

She smiled and nodded slightly. Her eyes looked to the side, as though sharing a little joke with herself. 'Kiss me again.'

~

They went back to the house, all ideas of lunch now firmly out the window. Gandalf sat at the end of the bed licking his paws while they lay on it, semi clothed, discovering each other's bodies with their hands and their mouths. It wasn't a frantic, passionate discovery, not like in the movies. It was a slow, tender and tentative discovery, like two people who wanted each other very much, but were all too aware of the silent presence of the dead friend that hung over them.

Ashley broke away from their kiss and shook her head. 'This is too soon.'

Kieran cast his eyes downward and nodded. 'Okay.'

'I'm sorry. I thought it would be all right. Doing this. I mean; I want it. I really do. It's just...'

'It's okay. I know. I suppose I feel the same. I'm just not as good at controlling it. It's been a long time for me.'

She eyed him quizzically. 'Really? How long?'

'Long enough.' Kieran forced a smile. He was trying to convince her that it didn't matter.

Ashley laid her head back on the pillow and looked up at the ceiling. 'I hope you don't mind waiting.'

Kieran shook his head. 'The best things in life are worth waiting for. Besides. For some reason, after I met you, the rest of the world seemed to stop existing.'

Ashley eyed him for a moment longer, then sat up and swung her legs round to sit on the side of the bed. She had her back to him. He watched her as she rubbed her eyes. Looking at the bedside table she saw his sleeping tablets and picked them up, rotating the bottle in her hand. 'Are these what the doctor gave to you for the sleeping problem?'

'Yes.'

'Do they work?'

Kieran shrugged as best he could given that he was resting on one elbow. 'I wish I knew.'

She put them back. 'How long have you been taking them?'

He reached over and picked up the bottle himself. 'Just over a month. Since the day after you loaned me the video camera.'

He opened the lid and saw there were about ten left inside. He screwed the lid back on and looked at the water-smudged label, which had blotted some of the letters, making it harder to read.

*Only for **u**se by **p**rescribed pat**i**ent. Not to be taken by any other person. Tak**e** one **c**apsule at le**a**st one hour before sleep - Dr Thro**w**er.*

'You should stop taking them,' said Ashley. 'It can't be good for you. Indefinitely taking tablets like this when you can't directly see the benefits.'

Kieran put the bottle back on the bedside table. 'You're probably right. What I should really do is finish off the tablets like the doctor ordered, then perhaps I should try more natural remedies. Cutting out caffeine. Drink camomile tea.'

She got up and headed for the bedroom door. 'And get more exercise too.'

'Are you saying I'm fat?'

'No. You need to make yourself more tired. Hold on I need the loo.'

Kieran listened to her walking down the hall to the bathroom, go in and close the door.

'Gandalf, what do you think of her?'

Gandalf ignored him and carried on cleaning his inner thigh. Kieran reached down and stroked Gandalf's little cat-shaped head.

'C'mon. Don't you think she's a babe?'

Kieran heard the toilet flush. He lay back and stared out the window at the dark blue sky that he could see through the jagged branches of the trees. She came back into the bedroom.

'Don't you hate it when it gets dark this early,' he said. 'It's only four o'clock.'

'I was thinking about Edward Gosnell,' she said as she lay back on the bed.

'In what way?'

'I was thinking about how he murdered three men just to protect his wife. It made me think that we all have capacity to murder people, if someone we love is threatened.'

'Do you think so?'

She shifted herself onto her side, 'Of course. I mean, if someone broke into my house and threatened to kill a member of my family, and it came right down to it, as an act of defense, I wouldn't hesitate to kill in order to defend them, y'know.'

'I suppose you're right. Everyone probably has a line; a breaking point, if it really came to it.'

'On the whole I think Gosnell's sentiments were right. His reaction to the threat on his wife was chivalrous, even though it was extreme. I'd certainly be glad to know that I had a man that would... y'know, defend my honour.'

20

The day has come for us to wash the train carriages, as ordered by the Kommandant. I look along the side of the train, which is now empty of Jews. They are all now standing on the Rampe, waiting for the order to move into the Camp. I know what lies ahead for them. The separation. The humiliation. The death.

I am standing near the last boxcar. I am holding a bucket of cold soapy water and a cloth. I am waiting for the order to start cleaning. I am watching a Nazi guard further down towards the front. He is swinging a baby against the side of the train, smashing its head against the riveted steel. I recognise the guard as Erich Bauer, the guard who snatched my wife's necklace. Beside him, a thin young woman lies curled up in a ball on the ground. Another guard is kicking her. I don't know what she has done to anger them. Often it seems like they barely need an excuse to do what they do.

One of the guards near the entrance to the camp bellows the order to move, and, with shouts of encouragement from the other guards stationed along the line, the Jews march into the camp. As I look at them I am reminded of the day I arrived at Sobibor. I know that many of the people I am watching now will not be alive tomorrow.

21

They say that Spring is never Spring unless it comes early. Well, Spring was definitely Spring that year. By mid-February crocuses had clustered in patches on the lawns in front of people's houses and the yellowest of happy daffodils helped the drab departing winter on its way by introducing some much-needed colour to the frame.

The sunshine that month was making promises of being warm, and as it traversed the sky at such an acute late-winter angle it pierced the world rather than just illuminate it.

Over this time Ashley and Kieran spent more and more time together. They occasionally slept in Kieran's bed. They often held hands in the street. She would sometimes steal his clothes to wear to work. She cooked for him. He gave her a set of keys.

Was it right? This was a question Kieran posed to himself several times during the first two months since they kissed at New Year. He was never able to fully resolve it in his mind, and he was never entirely sure about how Ashley had chosen to deal with it. But one thing he had noticed was that after New Year, she seemed to have banished some clouds from her life. Whether it was caused by their kiss and subsequent encounters, or whether it was just a New Year's resolution for her to brush away the cobwebs of her terrible previous year, Kieran couldn't be sure. Regardless of the reasons and their causes, he knew he was happy, and she seemed happy too.

It didn't stop them thinking about Phillip though. They talked about him sometimes and would always be ready to raise a glass to their absent friend. Kieran even wondered if Phillip's death was part of the universe's grand machinations to bring Ashley and him together, though he never articulated that particular thought to her.

The fourth day of March was Ashley's birthday, and Kieran booked a table at his favourite Thai restaurant, the Blue Elephant in Fulham Broadway. He had raved about it enough

SPIRECLAW

times and she had always wanted to go. It was going to be expensive, but Ashley was special and the food was nothing short of fabulous.

Up until the coffee, all they had talked about was the food and how good it was, but once all the plates had been taken away, the conversation turned to other things.

'It's been a while since we talked about Spireclaw,' Ashley said, sipping her coffee and putting it back down because it was too hot.

Kieran nodded. 'You're right. It's like we've moved on from all that.'

'I think it's because we ran out of ideas. We lost our direction with it.'

'It was a healthy diversion.'

'It was a surreal diversion.'

'And a healthy diversion, to take our minds off Phillip.'

'Did we exhaust all our options?'

'Yes I think we did.'

Ashley tried her coffee again, taking a bigger sip this time. 'What about the churches?'

'What about the churches?'

'The Spireclaw waypoint churches. It occurred to me that we never went to see them.'

Kieran smirked. 'Why would they even... Do you think we should? What would we be looking for?'

'We didn't know what we were looking for when we went to Crown Passage, but it paid off didn't it? Maybe we need to try a leap of faith with the churches too. If you connect up all the dots, it's the next logical... dot! The séance led us to Crown Passage, where Ernest gave us that clue.'

'Do you think so? Ashley, why didn't you mention this earlier? It's been months since we went to Crown Passage. I'd practically forgotten all about Spireclaw.'

'I didn't realise it was up to me to mention it. Besides, it didn't even occur to me till now.'

~

It was a humid Sunday, and scattered clouds above threatened rain, but the patches of blue promised a finer day ahead. Looking at the sky Kieran saw that it could go either way. He decided to take his raincoat just in case the heavens opened. Into the pocket of the raincoat he placed the Duxford Museum documents, which contained the names of the waypoint churches, just in case he might need them.

Ashley had borrowed her father's silver Ford Mondeo and picked him up at ten in the morning. He jumped into the passenger seat and threw his coat on the back seat. It landed on top of a picnic cooler.

Kieran looked at Ashley. She was smiling broadly. 'You're perfect Ashley.'

'Thanks babe.'

Ashley had printed out maps and directions off the Internet and they drove for about forty minutes to get to Buckhurst Hill, listening to Radio One the whole way. Thankfully the Sunday traffic wasn't too bad.

St John's Church stood atop the hill next to a school on the main road. It was a pretty building made of irregular grey stone bricks, and beautiful ornate stained-glass windows arranged in sets of three. At the base of each of the walls were blossoming flowerbeds that fuelled the fresh springtime feeling, and young trees in the grounds were starting to turn green and lose their bony winter look.

Ashley swung the Mondeo into a parking space just outside the gate and they got out.

Kieran looked up at the church's pointed spire and tried to imagine what it would be like to see Spitfires flying overhead. It was a difficult picture to conjure, being so far removed from anything he'd ever know. He found it helped if he pretended he was looking at the world in black-and-white. That idea brought a smile to his lips.

They went through the gate into the grounds. A cluster of people were hanging around the main door to the church. Children were running around on the grass. It seemed that a morning service had just ended.

SPIRECLAW

'Ashley, I can't really imagine what we're looking for now. I mean. We know what Spireclaw is. We know how it relates to these churches. What are we looking for?'

Ashley, who was wearing her sunglasses in her hair, dropped them over her eyes and shielded her eyes from the sun. She was scanning the grounds. 'Do you reckon Edward Gosnell is buried here?'

'Eh? I thought Edward Gosnell was the yank who…'

'But we're not sure about that are we? There may be other Edward Gosnells that once lived around here, and the one we're looking for could be buried right here, or at one of the other churches.'

Around the back of the church, in the cold shade cast by the tall spire, they looked at gravestones. Grey slabs of angular overgrown and mossy old stone that marked the passing of life after life through the parish. Holding hands they regarded name after name, carved into the stone along with dates and the names of surviving relatives.

None of the names they saw meant anything to either of them.

'Shall we go on to the next church?' said Kieran.

'Okay.'

~

The Essendon Church spire was short and stubby. It sat atop the square main building, and Kieran wondered if it had changed much over the last sixty or so years since Ernest's plane swooped over it on its way to Duxford.

'I can't imagine that this was a particularly good waypoint,' said Kieran squinting up at the spire as they walked along the concrete paths that weaved in and out of the Hatfield gravestones.

'It worked though, didn't it.'

'Ernest Clarke must have been an exceptional pilot.'

'I don't doubt that for a minute. He'd been flying a long time before the war started, and they must have known he was good enough, otherwise they wouldn't have let him fly.'

Kieran nodded. 'I'm not feeling anything though.'

Ashley weaved her arm around his waist. 'Feeling what?'

Kieran put his arm around her too, touching the top of her arm where her little blue t-shirt became soft fair skin. 'At Crown Passage I felt this vibe. I told you about it. Like a magnetic, electric force. I can't really describe it. It was a just a sensation. But I just don't feel it here.'

'Did you feel it at the last church?'

Kieran stopped and turned to face her, his arm slipping across her warm back and down her arm to rest at her waist. She dug her hands into the pockets of his jeans.

'No I didn't,' he said. 'It all sounds ridiculous doesn't it?'

Ashley averted his gaze a moment. Then she said, 'Yes it does sound totally ridiculous,' and giggled. 'I think we should have you locked up.'

'Hang on, this was your idea!' laughing also.

She rested her head against his chest. 'Shall we have our picnic now, or go on to Saffron Walden and have it there?'

'Well that depends,' said Kieran, smiling broadly.

She looked up and answered with mock exasperation. 'On what exactly?'

'On whether you give me a kiss or not.'

~

Saffron Walden was only a stone's throw from Duxford, and St Mary's Church was the most beautiful of all the waypoint churches

'I could live in a place like this,' said Ashley as they carried the picnic cooler past the tudor buildings on the main street that led up to the church.

'I bet a house in this village would cost a bit though.'

'Well it's impossible to afford a place anywhere in this country.'

'I'm not ready for all that stuff yet.'

'Me neither.'

~

SPIRECLAW

Ashley Henderson was standing on the path looking at a gravestone that bore the name Mary Henderson. Next to the Mary Henderson gravestone was a stone bearing the name Drummond Appleby.

Kieran caught up with her on the path, put his arm around her waist and looked at what she was looking at.

Mary Henderson's gravestone had been placed on top of her lifeless bones in the year 1912. Ninety or so years of English weathering had battered the stone into submission, so it leaned back at an angle, as though it hoped in the future to let any more wind and rain brush lightly over it, rather than hit it head on.

Drummond Appleby's stone by comparison was much newer, and bore the glossy shine of the more recent type of headstone. Drummond Appleby - the stone said – died suddenly in 1967 and left no surviving relatives.

'What do you think that means?' she said.

Kieran ran his free hand through his hair. 'I think it means that there are a lot of Appleby's in the world, just like there are a lot of Henderson's in the world too.'

She looked up at him. 'And Gosnell's.'

He nodded. 'Not so many Gosnell's I think. I don't see any Gosnell gravestones.'

'I know, I was just saying that it's not easy to know what we're looking for.'

'I think the solutions are more obvious.'

'What? More obvious than this?' said Ashley waving her arm at the stones. 'They're next to each other, in this church. An Appleby, buried next to a Henderson, in a Spireclaw waypoint church?'

Kieran shrugged. 'Just a coincidence. Besides. Since when did this become about your surname?'

'Everything else has been a coincidence Kieran. We discussed this when I found that Gosnell article in the US.'

'I'm beginning to think that if you look hard enough, you'll find coincidences anywhere. It's not so strange is it?'

'Then what did we come out here for if we weren't looking for coincidences.'

'I thought we were looking for answers.'

'And we've found nothing.'

'Except this,' Ashley said, pointing again at the gravestones.

Kieran looked across the cemetery. Sunlight was slicing its way through the trees that bordered the area. The harsh springtime beams landed in angular rhombuses on the stones, creating a cacophony of light and dark.

'Perhaps we should leave this thing be,' he said. 'We're beginning to differ about it, and I'd hate for us to get annoyed with each other about something so...'

Ashley grinned. 'Something so silly?'

Kieran smiled too. 'I was going to say... intangible.'

Ashley nodded and dug her hands into her pockets. 'I'm getting hungry now. How about you?'

'I'm positively starving! Let's eat, and maybe we can find somewhere to have tea.'

22

'Interview with Edward Gosnell commencing four-fifteen pm on March 23rd 1973. Present are arresting officer Carl Gardner and myself Officer Jay Meeks. Mr Gosnell would you confirm your date of birth.'

'Yes sir, October 14th 1943.'

'Thank you. Please describe the events of the evening of February 20th leading up to the incident.'

'That evening my wife and I drove out to the Holy Road truckstop to meet with some friends and have some dinner.'

'What time was that exactly?'

'When we left? Or when we got there?'

'Both'

'We musta left around eight, got there about nine. Somethin' like that.'

'And when you arrived at the truckstop did you see any of the men who you allege later attacked your wife?'

SPIRECLAW

'Brecker and Rosen were there, playing pool. I didn't really notice them at the time. They weren't botherin' no one, but later, later on I remembered that's what they was doin'. And thinkin' back on it, they were makin' eyes at Mandy, my wife, even before she went out to the parking lot.'

'And there was no sign of Jonathan Parry at this time.'

'No sir. I didn't see him arrive.'

'Were your friends already present at the truckstop when you and your wife arrived?'

'Yes they were.'

'And at what point during the meal did your wife go out to the parking lot?'

'The couple we were with, they'd invited me an' Mandy out to their farm the following weekend. We was all havin' a conversation about what was the quickest way to get out there. So Mandy went out to our pickup to get a map, to settle the discussion.'

'What happened next?'

'She didn't come back. That's what happened next.'

'How long did you wait before you went outside to look for her?'

'About fifteen minutes.'

'And at the time you went outside did you see Randy Brecker and Michael Rosen up at the pool table?'

'Huh, I know you're trying to catch me out sir. They weren't at the pool table when I went outside because they were already out in the parking lot trying to rape my wife.'

'Tell me what you saw when you got outside.'

'Well nothin' at first. All I saw at first was an empty parking lot. When I got to where my pickup was I didn't see Mandy so I started looking around. There were a few big trucks near the rear of the lot and I heard voices comin' from behind one of the vehicles.'

'Were the voices male or female.'

'A couple of male voices. So like I was sayin' I started to walk over there. I was gonna ask them if they'd seen my wife but when I got round there I saw all three of them.'

'Who did you see?'

'Parry, Rosen and Brecker They had my...'

'For the record the names are Jonathan Parry, Michael Rosen and Randy Brecker. Is that correct Mr Gosnell?'

'Yes sir. They had my wife down on the ground. Brecker and Rosen were holding her arms down. Rosen also had his hand over her mouth to stop her making any noise. Parry, he was standing over her. Messing with his button-flies.'

'Did they see you arrive?'

'No sir, they weren't keeping a good lookout at all. I came round the side of the truck and they were down the other end near the back wheels.'

'The vehicle in question was over thirty feet long. And the light at the rear of the parking lot had a broken bulb. How can you be sure which two were holding her arms?'

'Sir I ain't blind. I've seen those men before. I knew which one was which. And besides, I ain't denying that I shot 'em, so what difference does it make?'

'We're just trying to establish all the facts of the case Mr Gosnell. What did you do next?'

'Well I was fuckin' furious by now. I was gonna just shout at 'em to get off her y'know, but I reckoned they would've tried to mess me up for catchin' 'em. So I went back to my pickup and got my shotgun. Loaded it up. Went round the other side of the truck. Parry was about to fuck her. He was getting ready to y'know, go inside. They'd hitched up her goddam skirt.'

'What did you do next?'

'I shot him.'

'You shot Jonathan Parry.'

'Yes sir I shot him in the face. Then I emptied one into the back of Rosen's head before either of 'em had a chance to react. I took Brecker out last. Mandy crawled away under the truck until I finished shooting. Now. Before you say anything I just wanna say I don't regret what I did sir. Not for one minute.'

23

The Jews in the camp kitchen are whispering about a Jew called Leon Feldhendler. He has been talking about escaping. Feldhendler was the head of the Judenrat in the Zolkiewka Ghetto, and had to carry out Nazi orders against the Jews, forming forced labour battalions, and herding Jews out of the ghettos and onto the trains. I hear it is his intention to help all the Jews in Sobibor escape. At least, those in Camp I and Camp II. Those in Camp III cannot be saved. It is clear to us all that security in Camp III is too tight to break. All of us have decided to become part of Feldhendler's plan, because it is clear that if any of us are left behind after the escape, we will be killed.

Feldhendler has recruited another Jew named Alexander Pechersky, who was once a soldier and a leader of men. Such military leadership is needed if six hundred Jews are to escape a well-guarded camp without being taken down by machine guns. All the others trust Feldhendler, and therefore we trust his decision to enlist Pechersky.

Feldhendler has gathered us for a secret meeting in his hut. Those of us who are able to attend do so, and the meeting is conducted in hushed darkness.

'There are rumours among some of the prisoners here,' says Feldhendler, 'that there will be no more trains arriving at Sobibor. The last of the Jews to be sent here have already gone to he chambers in Camp III. This means only one thing. That Sobibor will close soon. With no camp, they will have no need for any Jews to run it. We will be sent to our deaths just like the others. So now that we face the gas chambers, we have nothing to lose by trying to escape. Pechersky and I have formulated a plan, which has only a small chance of succeeding. This is a poor probability, but we believe it is the best and only chance we have. I think I speak for all of us when I say that we are all ready to join an escape attempt. Pechersky. Please will you outline the plan.'

'Thank you . We want to make the break on October 13th, in three days time. This is what will happen. Malachi, Heshel and Ephraim. This is what I want you to do. At one o'clock in the *afternoon, you will start calling guards into the tailors shop for uniform fittings. One by one you will kill them, as silently as possible. You must hide the bodies. I will say this now as it is vital to our plan. No Jew should be forced to kill, but if any Jew is unable to carry out an order to kill he must be killed. If he spoils the plan he will be killed anyway. Better that it is by our hands than the German's. Also I will say this. If any Jew talks about the plan or threatens to talk about it, he must be killed, for the good of the plan, and the good of the rest of us who are escaping. This plan is too important to be foiled by any one of us. Does everyone understand me?'*

Everyone in the room nodded.

'Good. While they are doing that I want Jakob and Abraham to cut the telephone lines between Camp II and Camp I. You must cut the cable in two places. This will make it harder for them to fix. Next I want you to decommission the vehicles in the garage. Slash the tyres and cut the brake cables. Anything you like to ensure those vehicles to not run. This should be fairly easy as the garage is out of the way and will probably be unguarded when you get there. Now, once all the guards in Camp II are killed, I want Ilan and Gideon to put on the uniforms of the guards. In the meantime, I want you others to place any pieces of rope you can find, and wooden planks and digging materials at intervals along the perimeter fence. Most of the fields around the camp are mined. Although some of the mines are actually flares it is still very risky to exit the camp in any way other than the front gate, which is not mined at all. However, if all hell breaks loose - and when it does it will be every Jew for himself - then at least there will be tools available to make an escape through the fence if it becomes your only option. I have heard rumours that the fields behind the guard's barracks are not mined either, but I have been unable to verify that fact. There is every likelihood that the guards will try to capture the gate as soon as they realise what we are doing. I hope for all our sakes that we are already well on our way into the Parczew Forest before they even realise what we are doing. Is everyone with me so far?'

Everyone nodded.

'After Ilan and Gideon have put on the guard's uniform, we will wait for roll-call. Gideon will blow the whistle for roll-call and everyone must assemble as normal in the courtyard. Wear warm clothes, because after the roll-call we will march right up to the gate and straight out of Sobibor.'

24

It is a bright sunny morning and Graham Whyteleafe is driving fast up the A303 towards London. He is travelling back to London after attending a conference at Exeter University. He is cursing himself now because he should have driven back last night, but instead he'd ended up in the pub with one of the speakers from the conference, talking shop until he finally realised that he'd had far too much to drink and was in no fit state to drive home. After closing time he booked himself into a Bed & Breakfast, with the intention of skipping the breakfast and leaving for London by about 6am.

Now Graham is tired and hungover. The bright morning sun is burning holes in his eyes as it reflects up from the rain-washed tarmac. He is struggling to see well enough in advance the twists and turns in the road ahead. But he is a good driver.

Suddenly a Porsche is rapidly coming towards him in his lane. It is overtaking a slow tractor in the opposite lane. Graham sees the situation late because of the blinding sun and is just about to swerve onto the grass verge when the Porsche dips back into its own lane. It's a close shave.

'Lunatic!' Graham puts his hand on the horn and gives the other driver a stern beep. He slows the car a little as the adrenaline drains out of his system and he wonders what would happen if he actually had a car crash.

His mind turns to thoughts of his only son. Kieran is twelve now and he's turning into a bright boy, if a little shy. Perhaps the boy would be less shy if his parents had been able to make their marriage work. Lorraine and he had been young and - he was prepared to admit it - immature.

He smiles, and his mind turns to thoughts of the tape recording Pat and Arthur had made of Kieran when he was little more than a year old. He feels a wave of nostalgia hit him like an oncoming Porsche.

He reaches across to the glove compartment and flips it open, then turns his attention back to the road because there is a roundabout coming up.

When all on the road is safe and clear he looks down again to see a mess of cassettes. Some are in boxes, most aren't. He tries to remember what the tape looks like.

Another glance up at the road, then he starts to pull out some of the tapes, letting them drop down to the footwell, 'Where is it?' he mutters though gritted teeth.

He remembers being given the cassette by his mother at the bungalow a few years back, but he can't remember ever removing it from the car. As far as he is aware it had been in the car all along. His hand reaches deeper into the cluttered recesses of the glove compartment.

He hears the horn of the oncoming lorry too late. He looks up and sees he is in the wrong lane. An Eddie Stobart lorry is coming straight at him.

Every single nerve ending jolts to attention. He swerves to the left too abruptly. On the wet road the car goes into a skid, the rear of the red Cortina sliding out to the right. The rear right corner hits Eddie Stobart and spins the vehicle brutally quickly in the opposite direction. If he were to survive this part of the crash then the whiplash from this initial impact will put him in a neck brace for three months.

The car twists through one-eighty degrees. The Eddie Stobart lorry is beginning to slow down now. It travels far enough however for the front of the Cortina to disappear underneath its trailer. The bonnet fits under there perfectly, until the rear wheels of the lorry mount it on the passenger side like a tank and progress slowly and heavily over the front of the car, trapping and crushing his legs under the twisting metal.

If he were to survive this part of the crash, he will be confined to a hospital bed for two months having metal splints inserted into his shattered, deformed legs.

SPIRECLAW

The Eddie Stobart leans sideways onto the banked grass verge and comes to rest, the sound of metal against metal is excruciating to hear.

The red Cortina is now perfectly positioned to cause a multi-vehicle pile-up. It is straddling the centre line on the brow of a hill. A speeding Honda shoots over the brow and buries itself into the Cortina, rolling it sideways onto its roof, like some freakish fairground ride. The ground above Graham's inverted form presses the pathetically weak metal of the roof of the Cortina against the top his head.

If he were to survive this part of the crash he will be paralysed from the neck down, confined to a wheelchair for the rest of his life, forever cursing his tired, hungover, sun-blinded stupidity.

But the shattered windows have sent lethal shards of glass into the car. One such shard pierces his heart. Even if an ambulance had been within ten miles of the accident then he would have had a very low probability of pulling through. The nearest ambulance, as it happens, is twenty-five miles away.

Graham is lucky enough to be spared all those things. All those things that he would have to live through.

25

'Psychological assessment interview with Edward Gosnell commencing two-eleven pm on April 2nd 1973. Present are Officer Jay Meeks and myself Mary Slater. Mr Gosnell do you understand the purpose of this meeting?'

'Yes Ma'am. You're a shrink and you're here to decide whether I'm nuts or not.'

'When you shot Jonathan Parry, what was going through your mind?'

'I'm afraid I'm unable to access those thoughts.'

'Why's that?'

'I don't remember too much of it now.'

'Are you saying that you don't have any recollection of what you did that evening?'

'Oh, yes ma'am I do. What I'm saying is this. What I did was like an instinctive reaction. It came from the heart. There was no tangible thought to accompany it. I shot those men because they were trying to rape Mandy. That's all there is to it. I killed them to protect my wife. I killed in her honour ma'am. I've done it before, and I'll do it again.'

'You say you've done it before?'

'Yes ma'am.'

'When?'

'In my past life.'

'You...murdered in a past life?'

'That's what I said.'

'Can you tell me more about this past life?'

'I lived in Poland, during World War Two ma'am. My wife was killed in a German death camp. I was there too. But I escaped, and while was escaping I killed one of the men who ordered her to the gas chamber. I stuck him with a knife.'

'I see.'

'But I didn't survive the escape. Most of us died before we even made it to the forest near the camp. Fuckin' Nazis laid mines everywhere. I was shot in the back by a guard. In my past life I died on October 14th 1943. I can tell you now that the camp was secret. Not a single newspaper anywhere in the world would have printed the story of our escape on their front pages the day after we broke out, even though it was one of the most heroic things that anyone ever did during that war. Overcoming the fear of what those guards were capable of.'

'That day I was born as Edward Gosnell. And you can send me to the chair for what I did to those three men, but I will be born again, and I will always defend the honour of the woman I love. And I swear I will always kill any man that comes between us.'

Silence.

'I live by the words "Qedem 'ahab".'

Silence.

'I live by those words and I die by them too.'

Silence.

'Do you know what those words mean ma'am?'
'No I don't.'
Silence.
'It's Hebrew ma'am. It means eternal love.'

26

Approximately eighteen things were happening at once. The peas were coming to the boil. So was the gravy. The chicken needed to come out of the oven, because the roast parsnips and roast potatoes that were bathing in its fat were starting to get a little too crispy. Ashley was calling to him from the living room because there was something on the television she wanted him to see.

The phone was ringing. Kieran answered it.

'Hello?'

'Hello, could I please speak with Kieran? Kieran Whyteleafe?'

'Speaking. How can I help you?'

'Ah hello Kieran. I don't know if you remember me. We spoke some time ago. My name is Ernest Clarke.'

'Ernest. Yes of course I remember you. From the Red Lion in Crown Passage. Could you hold on just a moment? Ashley can you give me a hand? How are you keeping Ernest?'

'Good thank you. I thought I'd lost your telephone number. I don't remember so well these days. My mind isn't as sharp as it used to be. Fortunately my son Terry - you remember him?'

'Yes, yes.'

'He found the piece of paper you wrote it down on. Otherwise I wouldn't have been able to make this telephone call.'

Ashley came into the kitchen and started to work on the lunch, taking the peas off the boil and checking the oven.

'I'm glad you called,' Kieran continued. 'So what can I do you for?'

'Well son. You remember you asked me about Spireclaw? You asked me what it meant.'

'Yes, and you told me it was a manoeuvre to take five planes for repairs. During the Battle of Britain.'

'That's right. But there's something else.'

'Something else?'

'Something I didn't remember until now. Spireclaw wasn't just a manoeuvre. Well, it started off as that. But Squadron Leader Appleby. He's the one who came up with the name. He retired a few years later and built a bungalow on the south coast. Must have been the late 1940's. Spireclaw was the name of the bungalow. It was the name he gave it.'

Kieran nearly dropped the receiver. It took a moment for Ernest's words to sink in. 'Where on the south coast? Do you know which town.'

'It's a village. Selsey Bill. It's near Bognor Regis, just the other side of Chichester.'

'Do you have the address?'

'I'm sorry son, I don't. I never went down there myself.'

'Ernest, you've been a terrific help. You have no idea how helpful you've been.'

'Not a problem my friend. Perhaps one day you'll tell me what this is all about.'

'I will. I promise. Goodbye Ernest.'

'Goodbye then.'

Kieran hung up the phone. 'Ashley, you aren't going to believe this.'

Ashley had put out all the vegetables onto plates and was busy carving the chicken. 'Believe what?'

'That was Ernest, from the Red Lion.'

'And?'

'And Spireclaw wasn't just a manoeuvre. It's a bungalow on the south coast.'

Ashley stopped carving the chicken. 'A bungalow?'

'Yes. Squadron Leader Appleby, Ernest's err...'

'Squadron Leader.'

'Yeah, he retired to Selsey Bill and built a bungalow. He named it Spireclaw!'

Ashley, smiling from ear to ear, dropped the carving knife and fork onto the sideboard, launched herself across the kitchen and flung her arms around Kieran's neck. She kissed him on the mouth. 'That's totally great! So, when are we going?'

27

It is October 14th and yesterday's plan to escape has been put back a day. Feldhendler and Pechersky called off the escape because, to everyone's shock and surprise, a train full of SS guards has arrived. No one is sure why, and this has scared us and made our escape attempt much more difficult. The guards are still here today, but the secret of our plan will not stay secret for much longer on the lips of so many people. Either we escape, or the secret does.

I am in my workshop making bracelets when I receive news that the murders in Camp II have been successful. My heart leaps and starts to quicken. We are past the point of no return now. If the guards find out what we have done we will all be killed. I wiggle my toes inside my shoe and I can feel my wife's necklace. I am relieved to find that I still have it.

Some of the Jews are exchanging knowing winks in the yard. Secret signs that mean we share a common goal and we are ready to escape from this painful and terror-filled existence.

The whistle blows fifteen minutes before roll-call and again when it is time for roll-call to begin, and I shut my eyes and hope that it is Gideon in a guard's uniform who has blown it, not an SS guard.

Many of the Jews who are gathering in the yard for roll-call are unaware of Feldhendler's plan to escape, and I hope against hope that they will be able to adapt swiftly to the situation as it changes. But who knows. Many of them are weak from illness and malnutrition, and may not even know what day of the week it is. There is no doubt that many people will be killed today.

I walk across the yard and fall into line with the rest of the Jews. I look nervously up to the front of the line. Ilan stands there in a Kapo's uniform with a whistle in his hand and my heart soars. Thank God; the plan is working so far.

The Kapo are Jews who are appointed by the SS Guards to carry out their orders. Many Kapo are hated by the other Jews; they are viewed as traitors, but I know that those recruited as Kapo were given a fierce choice. Work for the SS Guards and carry out their tortuous orders against their fellow men, or die.

I steal a glance up to the watchtower where the Blackies look down over the whole camp. They seem relaxed and this reassures me that the murders in Camp II have been carried out successfully.

In my trouser pocket a kitchen knife burns a hole against my leg. It almost feels like it has an electric current passing through it as my leg is almost tingling with the sensation of its existence.

There is a heated discussion at the front of the line. Another Polish Kapo is shouting at Gideon, I think he is saying that the whistle has been blown too early, and that now they will be punished. Gideon pulls a knife and thrusts it into the belly of the shouting man.

And now it is impossible for there to be an orderly march to the gate. Gideon's choice was to let the man shout at him and thus attract the attention of the other guards, or silence him and thus reveal the plan to the lines of assembled Jews that stand here at roll-call.

He has chosen the lesser of two evils.

A machine gun opens fire behind us, and this is the beginning of the chaos.

Erich Bauer is firing into the line of Jews, knocking them flat with relentless bullets. Everyone scatters, in every direction. Hundreds start to surge for the main gate. This is no orderly march. This is a situation that is becoming more nightmarish and difficult to read with every passing second.

I follow the crowd towards the main gate. I am surrounded by the screaming and shouting of my comrades.

More guns open fire on us. The man running alongside me falls as he is shot in the knee and I cannot help but think that had he not been standing there then the bullet would have hit me; securing my fate for I would not be able to run, as he is unable to now, and he will die. I watch him fall, and he sends out an arm towards me before his face hits the mud.

I see a gang of Jews running behind the carpenters shop.

I look up and see the Blackies in the tower, silhouetted against the cruel cold grey sky. They are shooting at us with their Mausers.

The surging crowd knocks over a Ukrainian guard on his bicycle and he shouts at them 'Did you not hear the whistle you sons of bitches?'

Explosions, in the south field behind the carpenter's shop. The Jews that had escaped that way must have stepped on the mines.

Erich Bauer is running towards us. As he closes in I see another gang of Jews storming the armory on the opposite side of the yard. Erich Bauer sees where I am looking and sweeps his gun around to fire upon them. To him it is more important that he kills them than me.

My heart is pumping harder than it ever has and I wonder if I can get to him before he sees that I have sneaked up on him. I duck low so that my head is below the shoulder-line of the Jews around me and I cut through the crowd and make my way towards him.

The mud under our feet has become slippery and it is getting harder to stay standing up. I know that my life depends on the things I do or do not do in the next few moments and should I survive this I shall find myself encased in another life-or-death challenge.

Erich Bauer; that evil man who pulled the pendant from my wife's beautiful neck still has his back to me. He is emptying his gun into the wooden wall of the armory in the hope of assassinating the Jews inside. I do not know if he is succeeding with his shots, and neither does he.

I approach him from behind and run the knife deep into his kidneys. He automatically stops firing and, with a childlike gasp, drops the machine gun to the ground. I twist the knife and wrench it forward, spilling his insides out through the huge gash I have created in his side.

The words; 'Qedem 'ahab,' escape my lips, and an image of Henya in her younger days flashes across my mind's eye.

Erich Bauer is dead and I dive back into the crowd of Jews. Now I am heading for the gate.

The fences on either side of the gate have given way under the force of people trying to get out of the compound. Jews all around me are shouting "Run" and "Don't just stand there!" The German guards are bringing up the rear and I see that if I join the back of the throng which is trying to get out through the front I will probably be shot from behind.

I remember what Pechersky said about the rumour that the fields behind the guard's barracks were probably not mined. I decide to chance it, because the alternative is looking increasingly horrific.

When I arrive at the rear of the barracks I witness a group of Jews waiting to climb through a gap that has been cut low in the fence. On the ground near the rear wooden wall of the barracks is a pistol and I see that in their eagerness to escape, no-one has thought to pick it up. Perhaps they have not noticed it.

I grab the pistol and force it into my pocket. Then I join the back of the queue, anxiously looking left and right to ensure that no guard has spotted this secret escape route.

On the other side of the fence is a stretch of field that is about one-hundred metres deep. The field ends at the edge of the forest and I see several Jews crossing the field, placing their feet in exactly the spot where the person before them has trodden.

No mines have gone off yet so it seems that the rumours were true. But I can't help but ask myself the nagging question; if the German Guards deliberately didn't mine the field behind their compound then they must surely have intended it as a quick escape route in the event of a problem in the camp, such as an uprising. So why are there no Guards escaping now? Are they all dead?

I do not risk my life a moment longer, as lingering in this camp now is the same as signing my own certificate of death. I drop to the floor and crawl towards the gap in the chain-link fence. In front of me is a man who has collapsed in the ditch

SPIRECLAW

that has been carved by a hundred knees and feet climbing through. I push his buttocks, 'Come on! Get a move on!'

He moans and lifts his head out of the mud. He looks ahead at the forest across the field.

'Come on!' I say again, and in response he seems to summon up the energy to continue his slow shuffle through the gap.

I check behind me once more to see if anyone is coming. I can hear the shouting of the others near the main gate, and sporadic reports of Mauser fire accompanied by deathly screams.

Please God let me live through this!

The man in front of me is clear from the gap and he carries on crawling in the dirt. I follow him through, telling him that he needs to walk, or run if he is to escape.

He slowly gets to his feet, muddy face and straggled hair making him look like a cave dweller. I stand up too and push him ahead. 'Run for your life my friend.'

He seems too dazed and exhausted to obey my advice, so I push past him and start across the muddy, uneven field, taking care to place my feet in existing footprints lest there be undiscovered mines on this patch.

Yet I feel liberated. Even to be walking across a minefield outside of the camp - where the very next step I take could be my last - is a million times better than living inside Sobibor. Much better to know that if I were to tread on a mine and die, at least it would be instant, because even that is better than the two years I lived in fear of my life in Sobibor and the ghetto. Better that it is over quickly, than allow the Nazi guards the power of psychological torture over me.

I make it to the edge of the forest. Others have made it too and are disappearing into the dark camouflage of the October trees. I see my comrades dashing back and forth, looking for the best way to head deeper into the cover of the woods.

A single rifle shot. I feel it slice my back, knocking the wind out of my very existence and I falter in my step.

Behind me in the distance towards the camp I hear laughter and shouting. 'Sie erhalten, gibt es kein Entweichen!'

I twist around as I fall and see the guard behind the chain-link fence waving his rifle at me. I feel the cold creeping into my veins, as though no amount of clothing could spare me from the chill that grows from within. My body hits the ground and my head hits the wet mud and the greyness of the world pushes in from the corners of all my senses. The guard sends another bullet towards me and I hear it echoing along a dark unforgiving corridor. It misses me, flying over my head.

I look up at the angular shapes of light and dark branching cuts that form the canopy of trees above my head. The cold slices deep into everything I feel and all my attention is focussed not on the stopping of my heart but on the small stone-like sensation in my shoe. It is not a stone is it? It is Henya. No, it is the representation of our eternal love.

Qedem 'ahab.

At least perhaps in some way I have avenged her brutal death when I killed Erich Bauer. At least I will get to see her now.

28

Kieran collected the rental car from a small outfit on the Uxbridge Avenue when the place opened at nine in the morning that sunny Saturday. It was the May Day bank holiday weekend, and all the weather forecasts had predicted a glorious cloudless weekend ahead. The car was a nice new smelling Vauxhall Vectra in racing green. He drove it back to his flat to collect his overnight bag. He also picked up a copy of the old wartime newspaper, the photocopy of the Edward Gosnell cutting Ashley had brought back from the States, and the audio cassette that he had found in the archive box. He had no idea if he would need any of them, but it was better to have and not need, than need and not have. By nine thirty he was parked up outside Ashley's house. As he switched off the engine he looked up at her bedroom window and saw her already waving at him. He watched as she turned away

SPIRECLAW

hurriedly. Within a minute she was trotting down the front steps outside her front door wearing a t-shirt and shorts, a small blue weekend bag slung over her shoulder and her sunglasses resting in her hair above her forehead.

She ran around the car, opened the door and jumped into the passenger seat Kieran found himself focusing on the weave of the fabric in her t-shirt, and once he finally saw its shape, he felt in some way that he'd glimpsed a part of her that she wasn't intending to reveal.

She threw her bag in the back and put on her seatbelt. 'Spireclaw here we come!'

Kieran grinned. 'You don't know how great it is to hear you say that.'

'Yes I do babe. That's why I said it. Nice car by the way. Was it expensive?'

He turned the key in the ignition. 'I'm a lowly postman Ashley. I'm afraid I don't do expensive.'

They headed into London on the M4, turning south at Hammersmith onto Fulham Palace Road, over the Thames and through Putney onto the A3. The traffic was on their side, and by ten-thirty they were the other side of Guildford.

Neither of them had had anything to eat yet, so they stopped at a Little Chef and ordered a couple of distinctly bland cooked breakfasts. At least they filled a hole, and enabled the two of them to turn their mind away from their stomachs to the question of how the rest of the day might pan out.

'How are we going to find out where Spireclaw is?' said Ashley, sipping her second cup of coffee. 'I'm sure that Selsey Bill has quite a lot of houses.'

'Unfortunately Ernest couldn't be specific about it. We can only hope that the name is written on the house, on a placard, and that if we cover enough roads in the car we should eventually spot it. If we're unlucky and the house doesn't have a placard, then I don't really know what we can do. Maybe we can ask some of the locals.'

'If we have to resort to that we'll definitely be reaching, don't you think?'

'Absolutely. Let's hope it doesn't come to that.'

They paid for their breakfasts and were soon back in the car, heading south.

The countryside they found themselves in after they parted company with the A3 was lush and green. The roads were sun-dappled through canopies of trees. The smell through the open windows brought back memories of long summer afternoons spent sitting in other people's gardens, smelling freshly cut grass and flowers.

They drove through Petworth and Midhurst, following long stone walls that bordered huge unseen estates.

Once they reached the ring road that bypassed Chichester, Kieran started to feel ill. Familiarity was edging its way into the corners of his mind, and it was creating an unsettled sensation in the pit of his stomach that he was beginning to find uncomfortable. 'I've been down this way before.'

'Have you?'

'It's a weird feeling because I'm really struggling to remember when and why, but the more I think about it the more I know that this road is familiar.' He pointed out of the window, half looking and half keeping his eyes on the road. 'That's Chichester Cathedral. I've seen it before.'

'Maybe in a picture.'

'No, in real life. My Dad took me to the seaside a couple of times to see my grandparents before they moved to Canada. I was about five or six. I always thought they lived out towards Southend, Clacton-on-Sea. Somewhere round there. But now I'm beginning to wonder. Perhaps I got Southend mixed up with the south coast.'

'Why did your grandparents move to Canada?'

'When my father died, they were pretty cut up about it.'

'I can understand.'

'I guess they wanted to get away from it, banish the memories.'

Ashley was staring at him. 'Do you think it might mean something?'

'What?'

'That you recognise this place?'

Taking a road to the left off the ring-road, following a sign that pointed towards Hunston, Sidlesham, Norton, Selsey and

SPIRECLAW

Pagham Harbour, Kieran said. 'Can I answer that question when we get there?'

~

Half an hour later they were driving down Selsey High Street. Summer was in full swing in the little beach town, and rightly so; the day had turned into one of those freakish early summer days where a glimmer of a heat wave to come fills the inhabitants of Britain with hope that this might be a repeat of 1976 or 1995. Outside many of the shops, hanging up on the walls, were fully inflated dinghies of varying sizes. The yellow and black Sea Ranger III looked the most impressive, and Kieran found himself wanting one even now he was supposed to be a grown-up.

Children in t-shirts and shorts ran across the road holding ice-creams and cans of drink, causing cars to slow. Couples walked hand-in-hand looking in shop windows, or rotating wire racks of postcards that sat outside newsagent shops and second-hand bookstores.

Bunting had been strung up back and forth diagonally across the street, the little multicoloured triangles flapping in the wind. On the lampposts they were tied to, big signs advertised the annual Donkey Derby on the Selsey Football Ground to be held on the forthcoming Monday.

'Where do we start?' said Ashley.

'I'm thinking we should head through town towards the beach. If Squadron Leader Appleby retired down here then he wanted to be near the sea. So I'm guessing that the roads near the beach are definitely the best place to start.'

At the end of the high street nearest to the sea, the shops petered out and were replaced with guest houses. The bunting stopped, and with it the activity.

'Start looking for Spireclaw,' said Kieran, weaving the car out from behind a green single-decker bus that had stopped to let off some children.

'I'm looking,' said Ashley, checking the houses on the left after they passed the bus.

'Check my side too, I need to keep my eyes on the road.'

Ashley looked out of both windows. 'Most of these places are numbered Kieran. I mean, they don't have names. I think we should try some of the smaller roads.'

'I can't remember if Ernest said it was a bungalow or not.'

'Most of the houses near the sea are bungalows.'

The high street terminated at the seafront, marked by a sea wall with a gap in it and a railing where steps led down to the beach. A little girl with huge sunglasses on with pink rims was standing at the top of the steps. She threw a frisbee down onto the unseen beach and quickly ran down after it. The road here met a T-junction. To the left and right were roads which ran along the beach, and opposite the beach, across the road on either side were bungalows, stretching away from them in either direction.

Kieran pulled over and parked the car at the side of the road. He turned off the ignition. As the sound of the hot engine ticked away, the rest of the silence was deafening after having heard the car's engine for the last couple of hours.

'Let's go and have a look around, shall we?'

They got out of the car and Ashley lowered her sunglasses from her head to her eyes, looked up at the clear blue sky and inhaled deeply. 'Oh it's nice to be out of town.'

'You're not wrong there.'

They crossed the road and stood on top of the low concrete sea wall. Below them on the beach, which was quite a good drop down, there were a number of young kids throwing a frisbee back and forth. One of them was the girl. They were laughing and shouting without a care in the world.

'Don't you wish you were still like that?' said Ashley.

'More often than I should.' said Kieran.

'You're quite a nostalgic little bunny aren't you?'

Kieran took her hand and looked at her eyes. 'The past is very important to me. It's the only thing in my life that I can quantify. I can't control how the future will affect me, but the past is like going home.'

Ashley nodded, and tucked her hair that had been caught by the wind, behind her ear.

Kieran looked east along the coast. Breakers divided up the beach at regular intervals, and where they met the horizon,

SPIRECLAW

just around the tip of Selsey Bill, he could see the drop-ramp of a lifeboat station.

'Let's go this way.'

They got back into the hot car. 'First shop we come to I need to buy a drink,' said Ashley.

They drove slowly along the beach road towards the lifeboat station. As it was a quiet road, they both looked out of the window to the left. In many of the front gardens of the bungalows that faced the beach were children playing or adults sunbathing. Ashley read out the name of each house as they went past it. Houses with names like Thelassa, Sea Reach and The Hoo.

No sign of Spireclaw.

'I want to get another look at the beach,' said Kieran, and he parked the car.

Ashley pointed ahead. 'There's newsagent over there, do you want a drink?'

'Yeah, can you get me a can of coke?'

'Sure.' She jumped out of the car, and Kieran watched her back as she jogged towards the shop.

He made his way up to the concrete sea wall and jumped up onto it. Putting his hands in his pockets he inhaled the sea air. Seaweed mixed with fish and dry salty wind permeated his senses.

The tide was quite far out and the water's edge was almost still. The upper part of the beach was stony, but the stones became sand part way down, and the sand was scored by little tributaries and estuaries that led down to the water. Out to sea a speedboat was tearing its way across the horizon, bouncing on the waves like a skimming stone, the impacts with the water were delayed in reaching Kieran's ears. He looked at the lifeboat station.

He felt icy coldness against his hand. He looked round. Ashley was standing on the grass verge holding a can of coke against it. She was smiling up at him. He took the can. 'Thanks Ashley.'

She held up what was in her other hand. A little white paper bag. 'I haven't had these in ages.'

'What are they?'

She grinned and twisted and swung left and right like a child, her eyes squinting in the sun as she looked up at him, despite her sunglasses. 'A quarter of cola-cubes.'

'Ahh, neither have I. Not since I was a boy.' Kieran wrestled a cola-cube from the little bag. 'God, growing up is crap isn't it? All those bloody responsibilities. Why can't we be kids forever?'

He looked at the cola-cube for a moment, the quick hand of the wind ruffling his light brown hair, gusting and threatening to push him off the sea wall. He popped it into his mouth, savouring the taste of his youth.

Wrong side.

Kieran looked up at the lifeboat station, which was now just a few hundred metres away. The hulking pier of wooden struts, upon which sat a green corrugated metal house, looked vaguely familiar to him.

'I've been here before. I really think I have,' he whispered, gripping the cola-cube between his teeth.

'What?' said Ashley as she sucked loudly on her sweet.

'Okay. We're on the wrong side of that lifeboat station. I've seen it before. I've seen it from the other side.'

Kieran jumped off the wall and started down towards the car. Ashley followed behind.

'You're having another one of your Crown Passage moments, aren't you Kieran?'

'Possibly. I just want to get a look from the other side.'

They drove further along the road, past the lifeboat station and parked. Back on the sea wall again, standing in a gap in a long line of fishing caskets, he saw the lifeboat station this time from the opposite side and he knew he was onto something.

Ashley sat on the wall beside him. 'What d'ya reckon boss?'

The cola-cube, now a quarter of its original size, sat on his tongue, and the smell of it was coming in from behind his nostrils.

Children were playing with buckets and spades at the edge of the water. Things were beginning to click.

'My Dad brought me down here a few times when I was really young. I can only vaguely recall it, but now I'm standing here I... oh my God.'
'What is it?'
'I don't bloody believe it.'
'Kieran, you're freaking me out.'
'The cassette.'
Kieran jumped off the wall and nearly lost his footing on the grassy slope that led down to the road. He got into the car and hunted around for the cassette in his bag on the back seat. Ashley got in the passenger's side. Kieran found the cassette, opened the box and slipped the cassette into the car stereo.
He pressed play.
Nothing.
Ashley said: 'Turn the...'
Kieran turned the ignition.
The tape began to play.

~

After the leader, there is the sudden sound of a baby, uttering a long happy wavering noise that sounds like he or she is being bounced on someone's knee.
A man's voice speaks over the baby, 'Up and down, up and down.' The man sounds sort of middle aged, perhaps older.
Stop
'That's my grandad.' said Kieran. 'I recognise his voice. The baby is me.'
Kieran pressed Play again.
The man is making up a rhyme for the baby. 'Can-you see-the boats, out on-the sea? Can-you see-the boats?'
Now a woman's voice, she sounds middle aged too, and with no discernable accent, 'I've got to go up to the shops. We need milk and flour. I don't have enough to make this cake.'
Stop
'And that's my grandma.'
Play
'Okay Darling,' says the man.

She carries on, 'And I need hundreds-and-thousands. Now have I got enough Bourneville? Oh dear I'd better make a list.'

'No need to get in a flap my love there's plenty of time,' says the man in a calm, reassuring voice.

Strange unintelligible rumble noise, far away.

'Ooh look, look at that!' says the man.

Stop.

'Does that sound like a lifeboat being released to you?' said Kieran.

Ashley rubbed her forehead. 'Play it again.'

Rewind. Volume higher. Play.

'...et in a flap my love there's plenty of time,'

Strange unintelligible rumble noise, far away.

'Ooh look, look at that!' says the man.

Stop.

'Well it could be I suppose,' said Ashley.

Play.

'Where?'

'Over there. Between the houses. It's down.'

'Oh yes. Gosh I hope nothing's wrong.'

Stop.

'Well she says she hopes nothing's wrong, so it sort of makes sense I guess,' said Ashley.

Play.

'Beautiful. It's quite majestic when you see it like that isn't it? Not when you just...'

'Yes... yes...' she says dreamily, 'Anyway, I really must go. Shall I take him with me?'

'Yes, why not.'

There is a pause, then the man utters a strained sigh, like he is struggling to get out of his chair.

Stop.

Kieran looked around. 'My grandparents house was near here. One of the roads that leads away from the beach. I swear it Ashley. That's definitely them.'

'How can you be sure?'

Kieran's fingers were absently tapping the gearstick. He looked at Ashley and tried to piece together an answer for her.

SPIRECLAW

Then he looked out of the window, squinted at the sun and searched the world outside the car.

'To be honest Ashley I don't know. It's as though this cassette...' he tapped the car stereo. '...this cassette has been reluctant to reveal its secrets. But we've brought it home now. Brought it back to its home town, and now that it's here, it's playing its hand.'

Ashley stared out of the window beside her, looking at the bungalow they had parked in front of.

Kieran said: 'There are forces at work here Ashley, I'm telling you. Guardian Angels controlling us. Controlling me, sometimes in my sleep. Making me do things. Sending us places. The Red Lion. My childhood home. There's a purpose to all these things. The Guardian Angel has sent us on a trajectory, an arc that led to here. Maybe it doesn't end here, in the same way it didn't end in the Red Lion either, or at my old house.' He regarded her for a moment. 'You think I've gone mad don't you.'

She turned her head back to him. 'Why do you think that?'

'Because if I was you I would think I was mad too.'

She took his hand in both of hers, cradling it gently, and looked into his eyes. 'I don't think you're mad at all. I think you have hidden depths Kieran, but you're not mad. Now. Where do you think your grandparents lived?'

'Well. I don't know the name of the road. But if I'm right about this cassette, then my grandfather was able to see the lifeboat dropping into the sea from where he lived.'

'So let's take a walk up there, see if we can jog any memories.'

They got out of the car and walked towards the lifeboat station.

Directly opposite the station was a road called Lifeboat Way, leading inland.

'It's not this one. I'm almost certain it's the one we just passed.'

They retraced their steps to the previous road, Beach Drive. 'This is it. I remember it now. My grandfather took me up to the beach. We'd walk up this road and he'd sit on the wall while I...'

Kieran pinwheeled, turning and turning and trying to take it all in. Tears were filling his eyes. 'My Dad...'

Ashley took his hand and gripped it tightly They were standing in the middle of the road. There were no cars. 'Are you okay?'

'I'm getting all these sensations. Smells. Images. Feelings I haven't felt for a long long time. I can sense my Dad. He used to bring me down here and...'

Kieran was *there*. Aspects of age six existed all around him and within him. The smell of the cola-cube in his mouth. The shape of the streetlamps. The sound of seagulls and happy children shouting by the low-tide shoreline. The clear blue sky. The bungalows. Shapes so familiar to the coast. The distant buzz of a high flying propeller plane. Lawnmowers cutting their way through afternoon grass.

Pointing down Beach Drive Kieran said: 'Then it can only be that Spireclaw is my grandparents bungalow, that my Guardian Angel, that strange, bizarre, manipulative force has directed me to here. Using the tools of my subconcious, coincidence, luck and chance to bring me to the south coast of England.'

'Kieran...'

'And now we know where it is. Let's go and find out why.'

~

It wasn't difficult to find Spireclaw. Once the flow of events had started to carry him downstream, it was easy to find the estuary. The cola-cube had unlocked the door to his memories, and as they walked along Beach Road , the only thing that seemed different now was that he was taller.

The bungalow was just as he remembered. Overshadowed by an apple tree in the front garden, with horizontal wooden slats painted white many years before. The paint was breaking off to reveal the dark wood beneath.

The building was symmetrical. On either side of the central front door were bay windows. The curtains in each were drawn completely closed. There was no car in the driveway and the place looked abandoned.

SPIRECLAW

Beside the front door was a blue wooden placard. Written in ornate text in thin brushes of white paint was the name of the house.

'Hello Spireclaw,' said Kieran. 'How have you been after all these years?'

Ashley swung open the front gate and walked up to the front door.

'Wait Ashley. What are you going to say?'

Ashley stopped on the bottom concrete step of the three that led up to the front door. She looked at Kieran. 'I'm going to tell them the truth.'

'And what is the truth exactly? That I'm a lunatic who chases shadows?'

Ashley ignored him and knocked on the door.

They waited.

She knocked again.

Nothing.

'There's no-one here anyway,' she said, trotting back along the path to meet him at the gate. She tucked her hair behind her ears. 'What now?'

Kieran looked more closely at the house. He looked at the slope of the roof, the gutters and drainpipes. He looked at the neglected flower bed, overthrown by weeds and creeping vines that clawed their way up the outside of the bungalow all the way to the window.

One of the curtains moved.

Kieran's skin crawled. 'Shit. Someone's watching us from inside.'

Ashley, who was looking along the road, snapped her head round to look at Kieran. 'What?'

'Don't look now but the curtain moved. Right bay window.'

Ashley nodded. 'Okay, but why didn't they answer the door?'

'Beats me.'

'Shall we have a look round the back?'

'While they're watching us?'

'Kieran, we gave them a perfectly good opportunity to answer the door a minute ago.'

'Yeah but that still doesn't give us the right to go marching around in their back garden.' He looked at the curtain that had moved. It was now hanging still just as before. 'I mean, what the hell are we looking for anyway?'

Ashley took his hand. 'Come on babe.' She swung open the gate and pulled him through into the front garden. Then she let go of his hand and moved towards the left side of the house, where a gap between the house and the fence created a little alley that led through to the back garden.

They walked down the alley, over loosely laid paving slabs with weeds growing between and around them, past a frosted bathroom window, and into the small back garden.

The grass that made up most of the garden was waist high, and thorny rosebushes and chest high stinging nettles had taken hold of the garden from the borders by the high fences. A beautiful yellow butterfly was flapping it's way across the middle of the garden

'No-one lives here,' said Ashley. 'No-one would let their garden get like this if they lived here, surely.'

She stepped over some nettles and followed the path around the back of the house to some wooden steps that led up onto a small verandah. Ashley walked up the steps and peered in through the dusty window of the back door.

'Kitchen.' she whispered. 'It's totally empty. No fridge. No cooker.'

Kieran climbed the steps to join her, stepping over some empty plant pots that had been stacked inside each other.

Ashley tried the door handle. It was locked.

'Are you surprised?' said Kieran.

She bent down and looked left and right, stepping back and lifting the doormat she had been standing on.

Kieran lifted one of the plant pots, then another.

'Here.' He picked up the silver key and gave it to Ashley. She took it, placed it into the lock and turned it. There was a click and she pushed the door slowly and quietly open.

'Okay?' she said, looking at Kieran.

'We're going to get so incredibly arrested for this.'

SPIRECLAW

They stepped cross the threshold into the empty kitchen. Kieran was first hit by the musty smell. The smell of old dust. The smell of sub-basements. The smell of History.

Ashley called out into the depths of the house. 'Hello?'

Silence.

She stepped into the kitchen ahead of Kieran. He was hoping she was thinking the same thing he was; that their intrusion would look far less sinister if it was committed by a sweet young looking girl like Ashley. Better that any suspicious tenant would see her before they saw him. But then it was really beginning to look like Spireclaw was empty, and had been for quite some time.

Kieran opened a cupboard door. It creaked slightly and he winced and bit his lip. It was empty, and was probably once a food cupboard. A thick layer of dust surrounded circular imprints where cans and bottles had once stood.

Ashley took his hand and led him deeper into the house, out through the kitchen and off to the right along a very short corridor and into the living room. His hands were sweating, and she was shaking too.

The carpet in the living room had been removed, and only the underlay remained. Pictures had been taken off the walls and were nowhere to be seen, and the wallpaper around their empty spaces had faded in the sunlight, which now streamed in through tiny vertical gaps in the curtains, lancing down to the floor and catching every fine speck of dust that passed across them.

'There's nobody here,' whispered Ashley.

Kieran nodded, and shrugged. 'I don't know who it was at the window then.' He moved over to the window where he had seen the curtain stir.

'Did you see a person?' Ashley said, her voice only half whispering now.

'No.'

'Or just a hand, holding the curtain?'

Kieran shook his head, still whispering. 'I can't remember. No.'

'Could it have been the wind?'

Kieran looked around. 'I don't see any open windows, do you? Besides, it wasn't that kind of movement. It was pulled aside, from about halfway up. Someone was definitely moving it.'

Ashley buried her hands into the back pockets of her shorts, hunched up her shoulders and looked around the room. 'What shall we do now?'

'Let's look around, but I'd rather not stay here any longer than we need to.'

'I'm down with that. Do you actually recognise this place?'

Kieran nodded. 'I used to sleep in the little box room at the other end of the hall. Near the kitchen.'

'Shall we go and see?'

They walked back along the corridor.

The little bedroom was empty but for an old bunk-bed with no mattresses. A tiny dusty window looked out over the alleyway on the side of the house they didn't walk down. They moved on to the master bedroom at the rear of the house. It was totally empty, although the mere presence of old lives hung in the dusty, aged air.

'I don't know what's supposed to happen next,' said Kieran.

'How about we go back to the car and re-examine all the stuff you brought down. Maybe now we've seen this place something that we hadn't thought was important before might suddenly be more relevant.'

Kieran went back to the window in the living room where the curtain had moved. 'I wonder if this is where my grandfather was sitting, when he was bouncing me on his knee.'

He opened the curtain and looked up Beach Drive and saw the lifeboat station, nestled between two houses at the end of the road. Moving to the opposite bay window - the one on the other side of the front door - Kieran pushed the curtain to one side and looked out. He couldn't see the lifeboat station anymore. The gap between the two houses showed nothing but a patch of sea.

He moved back to the first window. 'This is where he sat when the recording was made. Now I can visualise the location, I need to listen to the rest of that tape.'

SPIRECLAW

They quietly let themselves out through the back door and walked around the side of the house, out through the front gate and along Beach Drive.

Back in the car, Kieran pressed play on the tape.

~

A few seconds of rustling. A door closing. It isn't an outside door though. It's inside, like a bedroom or a bathroom door.

The woman, whispering, 'Pass him here.' Then louder, to the baby, 'Hello little you.'

The man says, 'How long do you think you'll...'

'Ooh not long, just twenty minutes or so.'

More rustling, a floorboard creaking under the carpet.

She speaks again, 'See you later.'

'Bye love,' the man says.

A door slams shut. Footsteps dying away outside. A car door opening.

Inside, soft footsteps walking around.

Silence. The occasional deep breath. A cough.

A car driving off outside.

Rustling, then a flapping noise. The sound of wood scraping against wood.

A light thud, like the sound a wooden spoon would make if it were hit against a chopping board.

Fumbling, fumbling, fumbling. Another cough.

Recording stops.

'What do you reckon that sound is?' said Kieran.

Rewind. Stop. Play.

A car driving off outside.

Rustling, then a flapping noise. The sound of wood scraping against wood.

A light thud, like the sound a wooden spoon would make if it were hit against a chopping board.

Fumbling, fumbling, fumbling. Another cough.

Recording stops.

'I think it's a cupboard door closing in the kitchen,' said Kieran.

Ashley was shaking her head. 'It can't be. It's too loud; too well defined. The tape recorder is in the same room all the time. I think it's floorboards. She pressed the rewind button. Stop. 'Listen, you can hear the carpet being lifted.'

Play.

Rustling, then a flapping noise. The sound of wood scraping against wood.

A light thud, like the sound a wooden spoon would make if it were hit against a chopping board.

Stop.

'Okay,' said Kieran. 'That's a possibility.'

Ashley said. 'What I want to know is. How far are we going to take this?'

'What do you mean?'

She rested her head back on the seat. 'I mean, we've found Spireclaw. Isn't that what all this is all about? What I'm saying is, now that we've discovered that you used to visit this place as a child, do we really need to go back in there and rip up the floorboards?'

Kieran stared at her for a moment. 'I feel like I need to see everything through to its natural conclusion. Till we reach a dead end.'

'But what if there are no dead ends. If you look hard enough you will always find clues and coincidences in your life. This could go on forever if you let it.'

'Do you really think so?'

She tucked her hair behind her ears and looked down the road towards the beach. Then she said. 'I've been thinking.'

'Thinking what?'

'Well. What if *you* were the one who's been writing Spireclaw?' She let her words sink in before continuing. 'I mean, is it not possible that if you can have an entire dialog with David Everett - getting him to send you those boxes - in your sleep, then maybe you went down into your cellar and wrote Spireclaw down there.'

'And in the sub-basement at work? I hardly think...'

'Well, why not? Maybe this childhood memory has been firing in your brain, in your sleep, and these random things fall out.'

SPIRECLAW

Kieran thought for a moment. He examined his hands, tasted the remnants of cola-cube flavouring in his mouth. He knew deep down that Ashley could be right.

'Okay. I'm willing to accept that I might possibly - by the furthest stretch of the imagination - have written Spireclaw myself. But the question is why?'

'Like I said Kieran. Random misfiring of thoughts in the brain.'

Kieran could feel his throat closing up and tears forming behind his eyes. 'Can that really be all it is?'

Ashley took his hand. 'Let's go and sit on the beach for a bit. Try and figure it all out.'

~

They bought ice-creams from the newsagent and climbed down the steps to the beach, where they sat on the pebbles and looked out to sea. The tide was beginning to come in now, and where there were no waves before, little ones were forming and breaking on the sand.

'But where does Edward Gosnell fit into it?'

'Maybe he doesn't,' said Ashley.

'But the boxes.'

'Everyone has things in their life that they can't explain. Kieran.'

'Do they? I mean. Let's take you for example. What's happened in your life that you are unable to explain? Come on!'

Ashley stared at him. Her eyes darted between his, looking back and forth at his left and his right. She seemed to be searching for an answer. Tears welled in her eyes, and Kieran realised he'd got it wrong. She was wearing a look that said - how could you?

She stood up and started to walk off down the beach.

'Shit,' he whispered to himself, then got up and ran after her, recognizing his mistake and realising the need to appease her, just as he had on the day of Phillip's funeral, when he thought he was about to lose her through some other ill thought out statement. 'Ashley. I'm sorry. I wasn't thinking.'

He took her hand and she shook it off and carried on walking. 'You aren't the only one with puzzles Kieran.'

'Ashley!'

She carried on walking, her trainers crunching on the shingle.

'Ashley. I love you.'

She stopped, her back to him, and then she walked over to the nearest breaker and leaned against it, folding her arms. Kieran followed.

He was looking at her, and she looked out to sea, tears coursing down her cheeks. 'Since I met you I've been a new man. You've unlocked emotions in me that I didn't know were there. Do you remember when you came over to help me clean up that pigeon crap in my bathroom? New Years Day? Well when we did that, I was watching you in the bathroom and I remember thinking how special you were. How special you are. Ever since then I've thought, I want to be with this girl. I want to be with her for as long as she'll let me. And all the time I've been so scared that the only reason you liked me was because of my connection to Phillip.'

Ashley shook her head and turned her body more toward the breaker. 'To begin with that was true. But after a while...'

Kieran put his hand on her shoulder and eased her round to face him. Under her own initiative she continued the movement and ended it by putting her arms round him. They stood like that for a long time. Ten minutes, maybe not as much as that. All the while Kieran could smell the shampoo in her hair. He stared at one spot on the breaker; a knot in the dark wood. And all the time he could hear the waves starting to get louder and bigger as they fell gently on the shingle.

'Come on,' said Kieran. 'Let's make a compromise. If you let me look under the floorboards in that house, I promise that afterwards I will halt my investigation into Spireclaw, Edward Gosnell and the whole affair.'

Ashley pulled her head away and looked at him. Tears had reddened her eyes and although she was smiling and nodding, not all of the sadness had gone.

'It's a deal.'

Kieran smiled and turned towards the beach steps.

SPIRECLAW

'Kieran?' said Ashley.

He turned.

'I do love you too. But it's going to take a little while before everything's...y'know...'

He nodded. 'I know.'

They walked once again along Beach Drive towards Spireclaw, and Kieran was relieved to find the house was as they left it. Though why, after what looked like years of neglect, he thought it might have changed in the last ten minutes he had no idea.

Using the key on the back verandah, they let themselves in once again.

'I'm surprised this place hasn't even got a For Sale sign outside,' said Kieran.

'Yeah.'

'I mean, who does it belong to?'

They went into the living room and Kieran looked at the floor. The underlay had been cut in large squares and laid in tessellation. Kieran lifted one of the sections and examined the floorboards underneath. He ran his hands over them and felt the edges, yet none would lift up.

'Try somewhere else,' said Ashley.

Kieran laid the underlay back down and lifted up the adjacent section. The first floorboard he tried to lift came right up in his hands.

He looked up at Ashley, who crouched down to get better look at the hole Kieran had just created.

The black rectangle in the floor revealed nothing. It wasn't even possible to see what surface was below it.

'We could do with a torch right about now,' said Ashley.

Kieran plunged his hand into the hole and started to feel around for something, or anything that would validate his return trip to Spireclaw. He knew Ashley was looking for any reason to give up and go and find a Bed & Breakfast. But he wasn't feeling anything at all. Had he just opened a portal some alien dimension?

He reached further down and felt the muddy ground beneath the house. He was lying down on the floorboards now, his whole arm swallowed up by the hole, his cheek on the deck, trying to reach as far as he could in all directions.

'Nothing,' he said eventually. 'Not a bloody saus... oh... hang on...'

He felt cold rusty metal at the extreme of his reach. He felt around it. 'It's a box. A metal box. I'm trying to get a hold of it.'

He moved his fingers along one side of the box until they came to a handle, which he wrapped his index and middle finger around and started to pull towards him. It was big, and heavy, and Kieran knew he would have to lift out another floorboard if he was going to be able to get the box up into the room.

He stood up, tested the surrounding floorboards and found a loose one. Then another, then another. Eventually he had lifted enough floorboards to be able to climb all the way into the hole.

'I'm going to pass the box up to you, then you'll need to help me get out,' he said.

'Okay.'

He climbed in. It was just like being back home in Highfield Road. In the darkness he could see tiny strips and pinpoints of light between the wooden panels that surrounded all sides of the bungalow. The rest of the crawlspace seemed empty. He picked up the metal box and passed it up to Ashley's waiting hands. She took it and placed to one side, then offered her hand to Kieran.

'I think I'm okay,' he said, grabbing splintered floorboards on each side of the hole and levering himself up into the room.

He dusted his hands against his trousers and looked down at the box.

It was a rusty metal box about half the size of a briefcase and just as deep. It had been painted green once, many years ago but the painted surface had corroded and given in to rust. It was slightly battered and dented across the top.

'She's seen better days,' said Kieran. 'Go on, open it.'

Ashley flicked the latch on the front and opened the box. The lid was stopped at just beyond the vertical by two pieces of brown string.

SPIRECLAW

Inside was a stack of old letters. Kieran bent down and took the top one off the pile. It was addressed to: Arthur Whyteleafe, Spireclaw, Beach Drive, Selsey Bill, West Sussex.

Wednesday July 9th 1952
Dear Arthur,
Firstly I would like to thank you for looking after Spireclaw whilst I was away in Europe these past few months. You have shown your kindness and loyalty to me in many ways. You have treated her as though it was you who built her, not me, and for that I am truly grateful.
My time in Europe was sad. I spent a number of weeks in Warsaw and to see the devastation and ruin here brings home to me the full horror of the atrocities that were committed there. The destruction of such beautiful architecture (I had seen photographs taken before the war) made me wonder if we will ever see such wonderful and ornate design again. I fear not, because the cost of rebuilding is a factor and the sheer amount of work requires that corners must be cut. I was reassured somewhat by the enthusiasm of the people, and I am certain that the newly commissioned Palace of Culture and Science will be a stunning architectural monument to the future of Warsaw.
I feel a certain sense of pride that I was able to contribute to the liberation of that place in some small way, and that is the reason that my wife and I chose to visit.
I shall be returning from Liverpool in the next few days to discuss the other matter you mentioned in our telephone call.
Your dear friend,
Mark Appleby

Kieran finished reading the letter aloud.
'So Appleby and your grandfather knew each other,' said Ashley.
'Looks like it.' Kieran picked up the next letter on the pile.

Monday August 4th 1952
Dear Arthur,
Thank you for your card and flowers. I only wished you could have made it up to Liverpool for the funeral. Mother was always very fond of you, despite all the trouble we used to get into as children.

This sadness has caused my plans to change, and I have not been able to go down to Selsey as hoped. However, regarding the matter we discussed on the telephone, I have been carefully considering your request to buy Spireclaw and I am happy to say that your offer is most agreeable. Gwyneth and will be moving to Liverpool now to be near the rest of the family. We shall sort out the paperwork when I next get a chance to visit. I will write more soon when things are not so busy.

All the best to you and Pat
Mark Appleby

'So Squadron Leader Appleby sold Spireclaw to my grandad in 1952, or thereabouts.'

'It sounds like they were pals at school or something. What did your grandfather do during the war?'

'He was a newspaper photographer.'

'You don't think he took any of the pictures in the newspaper do you?'

Kieran shrugged. 'Go on, pull out another letter.'

14th April 1957
Dearest Arthur and Pat,
Thank you for your letter last month. It's wonderful to receive news of what's going on back home in England. Montreal is truly a wonderful place but it's not the same here. Thank you for the pictures of young Graham. He is a handsome boy and will no doubt grow into a fine figure of a man. You must be very proud of...

SPIRECLAW

'Oh my God, Kieran look at this.'

He stopped reading the letter and looked up at Ashley. She was holding a beautiful gold necklace, with a heart-shaped pendant resting in her hand on the end of the thin delicate chain, which was broken. She had the door of the pendant open and was looking inside it.

'What.' Kieran leaned over to see what had caused her mouth to hang open in awe.

On the inside of the door of the heart shaped pendant was an inscription that read

For Henya
Qedem 'ahab
Avraham
Warsaw, 1939

But it was the photograph that made Kieran's heart leap; the black-and-white photograph of the couple which had been placed behind glass inside the pendant.

It was a close-up of just their faces. He was a young man with a broad smile and warm eyes and short, dark brown hair and a thin face. She had dark brown shoulder-length hair and eyes that pierced the soul. She too had a smile that could banish clouds.

Ashley turned her eyes to Kieran and watched him looking at the photograph.

He said, 'Did you get this from inside the box?'

He saw her nodding out of the corner of his eye.

He looked at her, and she was looking at him in a way that he had never seen before. It was a look of pure release. She had tears in her eyes and she was wearing a smile that could banish clouds.

'Are you thinking what I'm thinking?' said Kieran, feeling the tears forming behind his eyes.

'Yes,' whispered Ashley. 'Of course I am. It's us!'

Kieran nodded slowly and looked at the photograph. It was like looking into a sepia mirror. There was no doubting the incredible likeness he and Ashley bore to the couple in the photograph.

'Do you... do you think it's possible that we...could have been married in a past life?'

Kieran looked around the room. He looked at the hole in the floorboards that opened into the dark crawlspace beneath. He thought about all the events that led them here.

He took her hand in his and said. 'After everything that's happened I'm beginning to believe that just about anything is possible.'

~

The sun was getting low in the sky as they left Spireclaw. Ashley locked the back door and placed the key back under the plant pot as they departed, walking in the long cold shadow around the side of the bungalow to the front gate.

They drove back the way they came, along the sea front towards Selsey High Street in search of a guesthouse. They found a double room in a place called The Marine Lodge, a reasonably cheap hotel with an en-suite bathroom, a kettle, and the tide-times drawing-pinned to the wall next to the fire safety instructions.

The room smelled musty, like Spireclaw did, only not as much. The covers on the bed were old but clean and the brown patterned wallpaper had probably been hung up sometime in the mid-seventies.

Ashley opened the window. They were on the second floor and had a good view of the sea and the setting sun. They took a shower together, washing off the dust of Spireclaw and in Kieran's case, the mud from the crawlspace beneath the house. Then they changed into fresh, clean clothes and set out along the East Beach towards the Pagham Harbour nature reserve.

Away from the windy beach, in the comparative stillness of the golden evening, midges danced in the thick air above the grass, catching each ray of sunlight as it tracked downwards through the trees.

They held hands.

'This is a perfect Saturday night,' said Kieran, feeling a favonian breeze brush his face.

Ashley put her head against his shoulder momentarily. 'It's lovely.'

Kieran put his hand into the pocket of his dockers. He pulled out the necklace and turned it over in his hand. 'For the first time in a long time I feel a sense of completeness. If it is possible that people live more than once then perhaps we have been reunited.'

'It's a nice thought.'

'I mean, it's a question of whether you believe or not. Is it possible that my Guardian Angel has been using the tools at its disposal to get me... get us to come to Spireclaw?'

Ashley looked up at him and he kissed her mouth. 'I prefer to think that it's true, that something is watching over us, pushing us in certain directions. Helping us make decisions in our life.'

He squeezed her hand a little tighter and kissed her warm hair. 'Now, what would you like for dinner?'

29

Kieran stands at the door and rings the bell. The street is silent because the hour is late. There is a light wind on this cold night and the trees are swaying, casting black silhouettes on the ground against the orange of the streetlamps.

Phillip opens the door. He is smiling. He says to Kieran that it is good to see him and the two of them go into the flat.

Nobody sees them.

Kieran is carrying the photograph of Phillip and Ashley in Fuerteventura. It sits in the inside left pocket of his jacket, and he can feel it there, as though it is burning a hole in his heart. Phillip would no doubt be surprised, and quite alarmed to find that Kieran was carrying the photo. But Kieran does not intend to tell him about it.

Kieran has something in the pocket of his cargo pants, and he keeps that quiet too.

Kieran takes a seat on the sofa in the living room as Phillip goes through to the kitchen to get a couple of Budweiser's from the fridge. Kieran waits patiently, looking casually around the room, taking in the modern tasteful décor of the living room, with pine floors and soft cream furniture and dimmer lights. He is careful not to touch anything.

He cracks a joke to keep the mood light, and talks about a drunken man he saw on the bus earlier in the evening. They both laugh.

Phillip returns to the living room and hands Kieran the open bottle of beer, then takes a seat on the other sofa. The television is on, and Phillip turns the volume down so they can talk.

They talk awhile about things they'd been up to. They laugh about things they'd done in the past. Phillip tells Kieran that it's really great that he just called up out of the blue and asked to come over, after nearly a year of not seeing each other.

Kieran nods and smiles. Yes, it really is great.

Phillip tells Kieran that he really must come over sometime soon for lunch or dinner when Ashley wasn't working at the studio. Then they could meet and it would be great. And maybe Ashley could introduce Kieran to one of her single mates.

Kieran nods again and continues smiling. Yes, it really would be great.

Phillip asks Kieran about his work and Kieran tells him all the little details of what makes his job in the post room so mundane. But at least it pays the bills eh?

This time it is Phillip's turn to nod.

After half an hour of chatting Kieran offers to get more beer from the fridge. Phillip points him in the vague direction of the kitchen and Kieran finds his way with ease. He collects a tea towel and uses it to open the door of the fridge. He takes out two bottles of Budweiser. Again, using the tea towel, he uses the bottle opener sitting on the worktop to open the beer.

He checks over his shoulder.

SPIRECLAW

He can hear that Phillip has turned the volume up on the television and is laughing along with a comedy programme. Kieran thinks he hears Basil Fawlty yelling at his hotel guests.

Kieran takes one of the Budweiser bottles and tips a third of the beer down the sink. Then he takes a small, trial-size bottle of window cleaning fluid out of the pocket of his cargo pants, and undoes the cap. Working calmly - he is pretty sure that Phillip won't come in - he fills the Budweiser bottle back up to the top with the window cleaning fluid and wipes away the spills with a cloth from the sink. Then he replaces the cap on the cleaning fluid and put it on the side, touching everything through the tea-towel.

Kieran spills a little of his own beer over the neck of Phillips beer bottle to wash away any residue of the cleaning fluid, and then takes both bottles with him back to the living room. He explains his delay away as taking an interest in the garden. The view from the kitchen looks nice, even in the dark.

Kieran watches Phillip as he drinks his last beer.

~

Phillip lies dead on the couch. He has been vomiting onto the seat next to him. It has taken him twenty minutes to expire.

Kieran unfolds a plastic bag from his back pocket and places three of the four bottles they've used into it. The fourth beer bottle remains in Phillip's dead hand. He wipes the bottle of cleaning fluid and places Phillip's prints on it, before carefully returning it to the kitchen sideboard.

Kieran is careful to wipe off any fingerprints after he touches the front door handle when he leaves.

It is after midnight. In the darkness of the street, Kieran whispers words he does not know when he is awake, and will never recall during daylight hours.

'Qedem 'ahab.'

Nobody sees him walk away from the house, momentarily disappearing under the shadows of the huge trees that line the quiet, suburban street.

Also by Huw Langridge

Duncan Schaefer is a chef in the Kuiper Mining Colony, at the edge of our solar system. He has become infected by a virus that is baffling science. With the help of his disfigured companion Maxan, he struggles to understand the physical changes his body is undergoing, which is earning him an unwanted celebrity status. Everyone wants a piece of him. Schaefer soon learns that the illness has a design of its own, and that there are greater things at stake than just his own life. Can he survive long enough to uncover the mystery of his illness, and make the connection between the physical changes in his body, and the future of mankind's place in the universe?

Schaefer's Integrity **is available to buy at all good online book stockists. ISBN 1849232245 - ISBN-13 9781849232241**

Also by Huw Langridge

Archer pitched his car into the outside lane of the motorway, London-bound. Accelerating to ease away the tension. Geek's inventions always pushed The Axiom Few into dangerous territory. It came with the job. And ultimately it was a case of "no guts no glory". They never wanted the glory, but they also didn't want any of their devices to fall into the wrong hands. It had never happened before and he'd always hoped they could keep things just the way he wanted. Secret. And revealed to others in only the method and measure that was to his preference.

The Axiom Few is a collection of eight short stories.

The Axiom Few is available to buy on Amazon and Lulu.com. ISBN 1446181960- ISBN-13 978-1446181966